Terror in the Night

A woman sat at the table with her back to us. Her long hair covered her shoulders.

At the sight of her, I felt my flesh begin to crawl. The way she was holding herself—face in hands, shoulders shaking as she wept—made her look uncannily like the ghost in the other room.

What was going on here?

After a moment Chris spoke up. "Can we help you?"

The woman cried out in surprise and turned in our direction. At the same time she reached for a light switch on the wall.

The lights came on.

Despite my effort not to, I cried out in horror. . . .

BRUCE COVILLE'S
BOOK OF

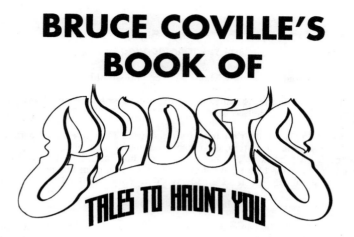

Compiled and edited by
Bruce Coville

Illustrated by
John Pierard

A GLC Book

AN
APPLE
PAPERBACK

SCHOLASTIC INC.
New York Toronto London Auckland Sydney

For Andrew Sigel,
my favorite noodge

ISBN 0-590-46160-5

10 9 8 7 6 5 4 3   4 5 6 7 8/9

Printed in the U.S.A.   40

First Scholastic printing September 1994

CONTENTS

INTRODUCTION:
RESTLESS SPIRITS

A formless mist hovers at the head of the stairs. . . .

The transparent image of a man in old-fashioned clothes floats down a hallway. . . .

The sound of weeping drifts from a dark and empty room. . . .

If you were to experience one of these signs of a ghost in your own home, it would probably terrify you.

But why?

After all, none of these things are actually threatening. Yet something about the very idea of encountering the spirit of someone who has died can make our scalps tingle and our flesh shiver.

Despite this terror, people *love* to read about ghosts. I suspect this is because ghosts bring us face-to-face with a question that haunts every human as much as any ghost ever haunted a house: *What happens after we die?*

And though they are inherently scary, ghosts

are also strangely comforting. After all, the idea of a ghost means that death is not the end, that there is something beyond the grave.

But what? That question gnaws at us, creating an interest in ghosts so great it is like a hunger. Indeed, it is almost as if something in the human mind *needs* to believe in ghosts, for we find the idea in almost every culture, every part of the world. (You might say that we humans are haunted by the *idea* of ghosts.)

Because I am a writer of ghost stories, everywhere I go kids ask me if I believe in ghosts myself.

The answer is both simple, and complicated.

The simple answer is, "Yes, I do." And while I have never seen a ghost—another question I am frequently asked—I am quite convinced that I once heard one.

(For a report from someone who *has* seen a ghost, check out Jim Macdonald's contribution to this book, "A True Story.")

But even if I didn't believe that ghosts walk the earth, I would believe in them. (See, I told you this was complicated!)

What I mean is I believe in ghosts as symbols of something else we all struggle with: the way the dead affect the living. For make no mistake about it—long after someone has died, the things they did in life linger on. I guarantee that the loves, hates, angers, sorrows, dreams, and deeds of ancestors far beyond even your great-great-grandparents echo down the years, shaping your life in ways you can barely understand.

In this way, we are all haunted.

Of course, if everyone who died became a ghost, the world would be clogged with restless spirits. It is not simply death that makes the kind of ghost you will meet in these tales. For a classic ghost story, there must be something that keeps the spirit bound to the earthly plane, rather than moving on as most do.

That something may be as simple as a ghost's unwillingness to admit that it is dead. More often, it is unfinished business of some sort: the need to right a great wrong, to take vengeance, or simply to say good-bye.

In the following stories you will meet a wide range of restless spirits, some frightening, some funny, some tragic. In all cases, the key to the story is the interaction of the living and the dead. For when the dead are restless, they can reach out from beyond the grave to touch our lives in ways both terrifying and wondrous.

So turn down the lights.

Settle into a comfortable spot.

And pay no attention to that person walking through your wall.

She's probably not interested in you at all.

Probably . . .

*Nina Tanleven and her friend Chris Gurley have a
gift for finding three things: ghosts, mysteries,
and trouble. They are two of my favorite characters
(I've written three books about them), and it was
a treat to find out what they had been up to while I
was off writing other stories.*

THE GHOST LET GO

Bruce Coville

I. A Dark and Stormy Night

Thunder rumbled overhead. A crack of lightning
split the midnight sky. My father said a word I
don't get to use.

"What's the matter, James?" asked Chris
Gurley. (My father's name is actually Henry, but
Chris and I were sitting in the back seat and pre-
tending he was our chauffeur, so we were calling
him James.)

"Nothing," Dad muttered as heavy drops
began to spatter the windshield. "I just wanted
to get back to Syracuse before this storm started.
I'm exhausted."

We were driving home from a Halloween storytelling performance put on by a couple of Dad's friends. I was thinking about their last story, the tale of "The Phantom Hitchhiker," when I spotted a woman walking along the road ahead of us.

I felt a shiver, as if the story was coming true. Then I decided I was being silly. But before I could suggest to Dad that maybe we should stop and offer the woman a ride, she turned and began running straight at us, waving her arms wildly. As she got closer I could see that she was screaming, and for a terrifying moment, I thought she was going to throw herself onto our hood.

"Dad, watch out!" I cried, even as he slammed his foot against the brake and wrenched the steering wheel to the right. We passed within inches of the woman. Through my window I caught a terrifying glimpse of her twisted, screaming face.

We were going too fast when we hit the side of the road, and next thing I knew we were bouncing down a steep bank. I realized with horror that we were going to roll over.

Everything seemed to slow down as the car went onto its side, then its top. When we stopped, I was hanging upside down in the dark, held in place by my seat belt. The radio had somehow gotten turned on, and a funny country and western song was blaring through the darkness.

"Nine!" cried my father. "Chris! Are you all right?"

"I think so," muttered Chris. I could tell from the sound of her voice that she was also upside down.

"I'm all right," I said. "Except for the blood rushing to my head."

I noticed that my voice was shaking.

"See if you can unhook your seat belts," said Dad.

I reached down with my hand. The car roof—which was now the floor—was only a couple of inches from my skull. Bracing myself, I fiddled with the seat belt. When I finally opened the buckle, I fell to the ceiling, landing on my head.

I heard a thump as Chris landed beside me. Between the music, the darkness, hanging upside down, and the terror of the accident, we were pretty confused. But after a few moments of crawling around on the ceiling, we got one of the doors open.

The rain was coming down so hard that within seconds my clothes were soaked and clinging to my skin. I was so relieved to be out of the car that I didn't really care.

After we finished checking to see if we really were all okay, my father said, "I'd like to get my hands on that dame. Do you think that was some sort of Halloween prank, or is she merely crazy?" He stopped, as if struck by what he had just said, and looked around nervously. "Where do you suppose she went, anyway?"

I looked around, too, but between the darkness and the rain, I probably couldn't have seen her if she was standing next to the nearest tree.

"You two keep your eyes open," ordered Dad. Muttering to himself, he turned his attention back to the car.

"How bad is it?" I asked.

"I won't know until I can get a better look at it," he said mournfully.

I felt bad for him. "The Golden Chariot," as he calls our car, is a 1959 Cadillac. It's huge (comparing it to a modern car is like comparing a seven-layer cake to an Oreo) and it's my father's pride and joy.

I could see why he would feel bitter toward the woman who had caused us to have the accident. It didn't occur to me at that point to think she might have been a ghost. After all, my father had seen her, too, and while by this time Chris and I had seen several ghosts, Dad had never seen any. It just wasn't something you expected of him.

"Well, we can't stand out here in the rain," he said. "We'd better see if we can find someplace where we can make a few phone calls."

"That may not be easy," said Chris.

She was right. We had been taking one of my father's famous "shortcuts" along an old country road, and I hadn't seen a house for the last two miles. Which meant we could either walk back two miles in the rain or keep going in the hope that we might find a house not far ahead of us. Since we were already soaked, we decided to gamble on going forward.

"Besides," said Dad, "maybe we'll run into that maniac, and I can give her a piece of my mind. Wait a minute while I get the flashlight."

Lying on his back, he managed to retrieve a flashlight from the glove compartment. Following his lead, we scrambled out of the ditch and up to the road. The rain was pelting down so hard that it hurt. We started out single file, but when we realized that there was zero traffic, we began walking side by side. I kept looking around, worrying that the woman might jump out of the bushes or something. What she had done already was so crazy there was no telling what else she might do.

Here's the first thing I learned that night: If you walk through freezing rain for twenty minutes, you'll probably be willing to knock on the door of a house you normally wouldn't go near on a bet—especially if there's no other house in sight. Of course, given how dark it was, "in sight" didn't amount to much in this case.

Actually, we didn't even see the house at first. Dad happened to play the beam of the flashlight over a mailbox. The name B. SMILEY was painted on the side.

"They've got to be kidding," said Chris.

"I don't care if Smiley shares the house with Dopey, Doc, and Grumpy," I replied, "as long as they let us in out of this rain."

We couldn't see the house from the road, but we found an unpaved driveway just past the mailbox. It was lined with trees whose branches met overhead, making it almost a tunnel. The branches provided a little relief from the storm, but the effect was so creepy I decided I would have preferred the rain.

Just before we left the tree-tunnel, a bolt of lightning showed us the house. It was about fifty feet ahead of us. Tall and brooding, it had a steep roof and a pair of spooky-looking garrets. It looked like something out of a nightmare, the kind of place you're *supposed* to find when your car breaks down on a cold, rainy night. The only light came from a single window on the second floor.

My father waited until the rumble of thunder had passed, then said, "Well . . . is it?"

What he meant was, "Is it haunted?"

This wasn't an unreasonable question. Chris and I had been growing increasingly sensitive to ghosts since we started seeing them a few months earlier, and sometimes we could tell if one was around just by looking at a place.

Sometimes, but not always.

"I can't tell," replied Chris, shouting to be heard above the sudden gust of wind that made the shutters on the house begin to bang.

"Me, either!" I bellowed.

I didn't bother to add that in my experience, people were a lot more dangerous than ghosts anyway. Not that I don't find ghosts eerie. Something about meeting the spirit of a person who has crossed into the world of the dead makes my flesh tingle no matter how many times it happens.

"Well, standing in the rain is stupid," said Dad at last. "Let's go."

Leaving the cover of the trees, he sprinted toward the porch. I don't know why he bothered to run, since we were already totally soaked. Maybe it was the nearness of shelter. Pointless or not, Chris and I ran after him.

The steps sagged beneath our weight as we dashed up to the porch. It was a relief to be out of the rain, even if it meant standing at the door of such a weird-looking place.

Dad stared at the door for a moment, but didn't make any move to summon the owner. "Don't be silly, Henry," he muttered at last. "It's just an old house in the country." He played the beam of the flashlight over the door frame until he found the doorbell button. He pushed it vigorously.

No one answered for a long time. I was wondering if we were going to have to start walking again when an old man's face appeared at the little window in the door. His expression was hard to read, and at first I thought he was going to turn around and leave us standing on the porch. But after a moment the door creaked open.

"Can I help you?" he asked.

His voice was scratchy, as if he didn't use it very often.

"We had an accident up the road a bit," said my father. "Could we use your phone, please?"

A strange expression flickered across the old man's face. It vanished almost immediately, as if he had caught himself telling a secret. His features froze into place, only his eyes betraying that something bothered him. With a shake of his head he said, "Don't have a phone."

My father sighed. "Is there anyone near here who *does* have a phone?" he asked.

The old man shook his head again, and I noticed that he was wearing a hearing aid. "No one near here at all."

"Any chance you could give us a ride?" asked Dad. He was sounding more desperate with each question.

Another shake of the head. "I don't drive anymore."

Dad looked back at the storm. He took a deep breath, then said, "I know it's a lot to ask, but could we possibly stay here for the night?"

It was the old man's turn to hesitate. He

9

studied the three of us for a moment, then nodded, and stepped aside so that we could enter.

His silence was spooky, but not as spooky as his house. The place looked like something from another time—or at least as if it hadn't been cleaned since some earlier period in history. Dust lay thick on every surface. Cobwebs tangled in the corners. The pattern on the carpet had nearly disappeared beneath ground-in dirt.

"My name is Henry Tanleven," said my father, extending his hand.

The old man looked at my father's hand as if he wasn't sure what he was supposed to do with it. Finally he took it in his own and said, "Benjamin Smiley."

"Pleased to meet you, Mr. Smiley," said my father. "And my apologies for intruding on you this way. This is my daughter, Nine, and her friend, Chris Gurley."

Mr. Smiley looked surprised by my name. "It's really Nina," I explained, as I did almost every time I first met someone. "People call me Nine because they like the way it sounds when you put it together with my last name."

Usually people take a second to figure out the joke, then smile and nod. Sometimes they start to smile *before* I explain, because they've already figured it out. Despite his name, Mr. Smiley looked as if he had no idea what a joke was. He just stared at me and said "Nine" in a flat voice.

Before I could think of what to say, an enormous clap of thunder shook the walls of the house.

The lights went out.

A terrifying screech ripped through the darkness.

II. Who Weeps by Night?

I shouted and reached for Chris. She was trying to grab me as well, and for a weird moment we sort of clawed at each other.

"Shut up!" yelled Mr. Smiley.

Was he yelling at us or at whoever had made the screech? If the latter, it didn't work, because the same voice shrieked, "Lights! Turn on the lights!"

"Stupid bird," muttered Mr. Smiley.

"Bird?" I asked in a small voice.

"It's my parrot, Commander Cody," he said in disgust. "He tends to get excited when the weather is rough."

At that moment the lights came back on.

"Thank you!" squawked the bird.

I felt a little safer. The bird was weird, but it was a normal kind of weird, if you know what I mean. Which was more than I could say for Benjamin Smiley. An air of deep sadness seemed to cling to him, and I felt that simply by knocking at his door we had done something terribly intrusive.

"Come along," he said. "I'll show you where you can sleep."

"Jeremiah!" squawked the bird as we started up the stairway. "Go to Jeremiah!"

We followed Mr. Smiley along a hallway where the pink and gray wallpaper had started to peel but was refusing to let go altogether. "You two can stay in here," he said, opening the door to a room that smelled dank and musty. He waved his hand to the right. "The bathroom is down the hall."

He flipped a switch, turning on a single bare bulb that hung from the ceiling. The bed itself, covered with a worn, pink chenille spread, was old and sagging. Given the circumstances, it was one of the most beautiful things I had ever seen.

"I'm glad we had already arranged for you to stay overnight with us," my father said to Chris. "At least your parents won't be worried about where you are."

"My parents always worry when I go someplace with Nine," replied Chris.

My father rolled his eyes. "I don't mind sleeping on a couch," he said, turning to Mr. Smiley. "I feel terrible troubling you like this."

"No need," said the old man gruffly. "You can use the room across the hall."

As soon as they were gone, Chris closed the door and said, "This whole thing is fishier than

Mrs. Paul's kitchen. Something very weird is going on here."

"I agree. Only I can't put my finger on anything specific. I mean, it's a little odd for the old guy to be living out here all alone, but lots of people are sort of odd. It just feels like there's something more. . . ."

"Didn't you recognize what happened to us out there?" she asked. "It was just like the last story we heard, the one about the phantom hitchhiker."

I shivered. "I was thinking about that one just before we had the accident," I admitted.

You probably know the story. A man is driving down a country road late at night and picks up a young female hitchhiker. Later—after the girl has either gotten out of the car or vanished, sometimes after asking him to deliver a message—he stops and has to stay with some people along the road. The man either describes the hitchhiker to his hosts, or spots her picture on the mantelpiece. A terrible look comes over his hosts' faces, and they tell him that his passenger was their daughter, who had died in a car crash many years earlier.

I saw a couple of problems as far as matching that story up with what we had just experienced. For one thing, the woman we saw hadn't been hitchhiking.

Chris nodded when I pointed this out. "But remember, in the story it's always a man traveling *alone* who spots the ghost. Maybe the fact that we were in the car with your dad kept her from trying to catch a ride with him."

"Also, we didn't spot anyone's picture on the mantel."

"No, but did you notice the look on Mr. Smiley's face when your father said we had had an accident? I bet he's heard *that* before!"

"So what are you saying? That we're trapped in the classic American ghost story?"

"I don't know *what* I'm saying," she replied. "Except that there's something weird going on around here."

I looked around the room. It was oddly bare. The only furniture besides the bed and bedstand was a low dresser with two items on top of it: a small lamp and a big old family Bible. I started to examine the Bible, but Chris called me to the closet instead.

"Take a look at this!" she whispered.

I went and stood beside her. The closet was filled with women's clothes, all of them old-fashioned.

Before I could think of what to say, we heard a knock at the door. Quickly Chris closed the closet.

"Who's there?" I called.

"It's me," said Mr. Smiley. "I brought you some towels."

It was an unexpected kindness, and I revised my opinion of the old man upward a couple of notches.

We turned out the light, then stripped and dried ourselves off. When we climbed into the old double bed, it creaked and groaned underneath us. The worn springs tended to roll us toward the middle.

"It's going to be a long night," whispered Chris.

"It already has been," I replied.

Given the night's excitement, I didn't know if I would be able to sleep or not. But exhaustion can work wonders, and it wasn't long before I nodded off.

It wasn't much longer before Chris woke me by nudging me in the ribs with her elbow. "Nine!" she hissed. "Listen!"

I listened.

The little hairs on the back of my neck stood up.

Somewhere below us a woman was crying.

Question number one: Should we stay where we were, or go investigate? The sensible thing to do was stay put.

Chris and I have never been accused of being sensible.

Even so, I wasn't sure we should go wandering around in Mr. Smiley's house. "He seems like an awfully cranky old guy," I whispered to Chris when we started to discuss the matter.

"You'd be cranky, too, if you had some woman crying her eyes out downstairs every night."

15

"What makes you think it happens every night?"

She shrugged. "Okay, once a month. Who knows? But if that's a ghost—and I bet it is—then I also bet she does it on a regular basis."

"Maybe he doesn't even hear it," I replied. "I bet he takes out his hearing aid at night."

"And your father is so exhausted he'll probably sleep right through it, too," said Chris. "Which means it's up to us to see what's wrong."

What could I say? Maybe this woman had been weeping down there every night for ages, waiting for someone to help her. Maybe fate had brought Chris and me here for that very purpose.

"All right." I sighed. "We'd better go take a look."

Question number two: Should we put on our clothes? They were still wet, and cold to boot. I was willing to wander around the house without permission, but I wasn't willing to do so naked. At least, not until I started to pull on my jeans. Then I had second thoughts.

"These are freezing!" I hissed.

We briefly considered the clothes in the closet. However, we decided that since (a) they might actually have belonged to the ghost, and (b) Mr. Smiley might catch us in them, we should leave them alone. In the end we went for the blankets. Well, I got the blanket. Chris got the pink chenille bedspread. She wasn't entirely happy about this, but the coin we tossed went my way, so there wasn't much she could say.

"I feel silly," I whispered. My teeth were still chattering, even though I was much warmer now that I was wrapped in the blanket.

"*You* feel silly," hissed Chris. "I'm the one dressed in Donna Reed's bedspread! Come on, we have to find that woman before she disappears. You never know how long a ghost is going to hang around."

With that, she grabbed my elbow and steered me toward the door.

"I wish we had a flashlight," I whispered as we stepped out into the dark hallway.

"Stop talking and listen," replied Chris.

The weeping was coming from right below us. Side by side, we headed down the stairwell.

The ghost was in the living room. We knew she was a ghost because even though there was no light—not even moonlight, since the storm was still going on—we could see her clearly. She was glowing softly, as if illuminated from within. We couldn't see her face—it was buried in her hands. She was sitting on the couch, leaning away from us, her shoulders shaking as if she was sobbing.

I assumed she was the woman we had seen walking in the storm. I would also have assumed that she was the one we had heard weeping, except for one thing: The sound wasn't coming from the ghost. It was coming from somewhere behind us.

Now what? Should we stay and watch the ghost or go and tend to the living?

Of course, we could have split up. But under the circumstances, it wasn't an idea that appealed to either of us.

The weeping was so heartbreaking that after a moment I whispered to Chris, "I think we'd better go see about that. I bet it's connected to the ghost."

Taking my arm, she led the way. We moved carefully, trying not to make any noise. Finally we reached an open doorway that led to the kitchen—something we figured out only because a tiny bulb in the top of the stove provided enough light to make out the major shapes in the room.

A woman sat at the table with her back to us. Her long hair covered her shoulders.

At the sight of her I felt my flesh begin to crawl. The way she was holding herself—face in hands, shoulders shaking as she wept—made her look uncannily like the ghost in the other room.

What was going on here?

After a moment Chris spoke up. "Can we help you?"

The woman cried out in surprise and turned in our direction. At the same time she reached for a light switch on the wall.

The lights came on.

Despite my effort not to, I cried out in horror at what I saw.

III. Dolores

The right side of the woman's face was normal—beautiful even. The left side, however, was hideously scarred, as if something had pulled at it, tugging the flesh toward her neck. Her eye, her cheek, the side of her mouth all twisted down, and thick ridges of scar tissue marched across her cheek and forehead like mountains on one of those three dimensional maps you see at museums.

"Who are you?" she hissed. "What are you doing here?"

Even as I was trying to find my voice, the woman was pulling her long hair over the side of her face, trying to mask the deformity. But the strands clung together, making bars down her face through which the scars still showed.

That was when I realized she was soaking wet. Glancing down, I saw a little puddle forming around her on the floor—water dripping from her clothes.

Was this the woman who had caused us to run off the road? It didn't seem likely that there would have been anyone else walking around in this weather but I had learned over the last

19

few months that when a situation starts getting this weird you can't take anything for granted. Still, she was the most likely candidate. It had been hard enough to see in the dark and the rain that we could easily have missed noticing her scars.

I wondered if she was dangerous.

"Who are you?" she repeated.

"My name is Nina Tanleven," I stammered. "This is my friend, Chris Gurley. We had an accident up the road, and we couldn't get help or a phone, so we're staying here for the night."

The woman made a little gasp. She had a terribly pained expression on her face. Before she could say anything, we heard a squawk from the other room.

"Don't go! Don't go!" cried Commander Cody.

The woman closed her one good eye and sighed.

Making a guess, I asked, "Is he talking to someone in particular?"

"Not unless you believe in ghosts," replied the woman.

"We do," said Chris. "In fact, we're sort of known for that."

The woman gave us an odd look. I could see an idea taking form in her head. "Are you those two kids I read about in the paper? The ones who solved the mystery at the Grand Theater?" Her voice was strangely eager. Even so, I was starting to feel a little more comfortable with her.

I nodded.

She shook her head. "I can't believe you ended up *here.*"

"Why not?" asked Chris.

"Because I need you so much," she said, starting to cry again.

Chris elbowed my ribs. "I told you so," she whispered.

Ignoring her gloating, I went to the table. "Mind if we sit down?" I asked quietly.

The woman shook her head.

I pulled out a chair and slipped into it. Tugging the blanket around my shoulders, I realized how odd Chris and I must have looked to her when she saw us standing there. I waited for the woman to calm down a little, then put my hand on her arm and whispered, "Why do you need us?"

"I have to tell my mother I'm sorry," she moaned.

"Was that your mother we saw in the living room?" asked Chris.

The woman sat up so straight that I thought her chair was going to fall over. *"You saw her!"* she hissed, her one good eye widening in astonishment.

I sighed, wishing Chris had waited a little bit longer before dropping that particular bombshell.

Chris nodded, adding, "She was crying, too."

Tears welled up in the woman's eyes again.

"Don't," I said, tightening my grip on her arm. "Tell us what's going on. Maybe we really can help."

And what if we can't? asked a little voice in the back of my head. I tried my best to ignore it.

The woman took a deep breath. Looking down at her hands, she whispered, "Twenty years ago this very night I killed my mother."

I felt my stomach twist. Were we sitting at the table with a homicidal maniac who might turn on us at any moment? I glanced around, hoping there were no butcher knives in easy reach, or anything like that.

"How?" asked Chris, who seemed to take this news more calmly than I did. Maybe that was because Chris's mother was still around, whereas I hadn't seen mine since the day she took off to "find her own life." Mothers were less of an issue for Chris.

The woman gave us a very sad smile. "I didn't shoot her, or anything like that. But I might as well have. I was supposed to go to a Halloween party with my boyfriend, Bud Hendricks. My mother didn't want me to go. 'That boy is no good, Dolores!' she kept saying. 'He'll only bring you grief.'

"We had a screaming battle, and she finally

forbid me to leave the house. When Bud showed up, she turned him away at the door."

Dolores sighed. "About eleven o'clock I snuck out. I had managed to call Bud, and he was planning to meet me a mile up the road so Mother wouldn't know what I was up to. She found out anyway, of course; she was brilliant at that kind of thing. And she went out after me. Dad was working late at his office, and Mom's car was in the shop, so she went on foot. That's how worried she was about me."

Dolores shivered. "When Bud picked me up, I realized that he had been drinking—which was one of the things Mom objected to about him. We started back toward town. The storm that had been building up all day cut loose. Bud was driving too fast, not paying enough attention. . . ."

Dolores started to cry again, but after a moment she got hold of herself. "My mother was walking toward us through the rain. I saw her first. I screamed and grabbed the steering wheel. We swerved, but not enough. We hit her, then went rolling into the ditch and smashed against a tree. That's when this happened," she said, pulling back the hair that covered her terrible scars.

No one said anything for a moment. Finally I touched her arm again. "What happened next?"

Dolores remained silent for a while. "I was

in a coma for about a month," she whispered at last. "When I came out, my father told me that both Bud and my mother were dead. He looked half dead himself." She turned away from us. "Dad never did recover from it all," she whispered, "though he took good care of me while I was recuperating. He couldn't tell me about my face, though, just couldn't bring himself to be the one to do it. One of the nurses had to hand me the mirror. . . ."

She choked on the memory. I watched her, glad that her telling the story had given me a chance to study her face, embarrassed that I wanted to study it, sick in my stomach from the way it looked. I wondered what it would be like to go through life that way.

She ran her fingers over the scars. "I don't mind them too much now," she said. "They seem like a fitting punishment. What I mind is what I did—that and the fact that I was never able to tell my mother how sorry I was, never got to take back my last words to her."

"Your last words?" asked Chris.

Dolores closed her eyes. "When we had our fight, I screamed that I hated her." She put her fingers against her scarred cheek, and I could see that they were trembling. " 'I hate you!' I screamed. 'I hate you! I hate you!' Then I ran upstairs and slammed the door to my room." She paused, swallowed hard, then whispered, "Those were the last words I ever said to her."

I shivered. It wasn't hard to see why Dolores wanted so much to say something to her mother. I know lots of kids who have told their parents they hated them, but none who had had the bad luck to have their parents die before they got to take the words back.

"Have you ever seen your mother's ghost?" asked Chris.

Dolores shook her head.

"Then why did you think she was still around?" I asked.

"Commander Cody sees her," said Dolores. She sounded defensive, as if she was daring me to contradict her.

It took me a moment to realize that she was talking about the parrot.

"How do you know?" asked Chris.

Dolores looked down at her hands. "He talks to her. He was her bird; she'd had him from before I was born." She smiled. "He always used to greet her when she walked into the room. 'Hello, Sweetie!' he would say. 'Hello, Sweetie!' "

Her smile faded, and she looked down at her hands. "The bird didn't say a word for six weeks after Mother died. Then one night after I came home from the hospital, I was sitting in the living room when Commander Cody let out an incredible squawk and cried, 'Hello, Sweetie!' "

Dolores's good eye grew very large as she remembered the night. " 'Mother?' I called. 'Mother, are you there?'

"I knew she was. But she didn't answer."

Dolores sat back in her chair. "She's haunted this house ever since. She comes about once a month. I never see her, but the bird always knows when she's here, always tells her hello, always cries 'Don't go! Don't go!' when she leaves, just like he did when she was alive."

She closed her eyes. "She must be so angry with me. I have to tell her how sorry I am. Maybe then her spirit can rest. I go out every year on this night, hoping maybe I will meet her along the road. But I never do."

She paused, then said, "I'm terribly sorry about your car. When I saw it tonight, I thought, I thought . . ."

She looked away for a moment, her shoulders trembling. "It's almost identical to the car Bud was driving that night. I thought . . . I don't know what I thought. I was so shocked I must have lost my mind for a moment. After you swerved away from me, I fainted. When I came to, I was horrified at what I had done. I went to see if you were all right, but you had already left. I'm so terribly sorry."

Now this was a situation my father had never anticipated when he chose to drive an antique car. While I was trying to figure out how he was going to react to this story, Chris said, "Do you want to try something?"

Dolores and I both spoke at the same time. "What?"

Chris looked a little nervous. "Before I tell you, you have to understand that there's a lot about this ghost stuff that Nine and I still don't understand. It does seem like the more we deal with them, the easier it gets for us to see them. The problem is, we're not the ones who need to see your mother. You are. But I'm wondering if we go into the living room and sit together, me on one side of you, Nine on the other, and hold hands—well, maybe it would bring you into the link so that you could see her, too."

The idea made me a little nervous; we had never actually tried to summon a ghost. And I wasn't sure what this ghost was going to be like. Just because she had been weeping when we saw her didn't mean she wasn't still in a screaming rage about what had happened twenty years ago. What would we do if she showed up angry? It's not like we had an instruction book with a chapter titled "How to Deal with a Really Furious Ghost."

On the other hand, I couldn't think of anything else to do. If fate had brought us here to help Dolores, this made as much sense as anything.

Dolores seemed to have pretty much the same reaction. "I'd do anything to see her again," she whispered.

"Shall we try it?" asked Chris, looking at me.

I nodded. Without another word the three of us stood and walked into the living room.

IV. What I Tell You Three Times Is True

"Jeremiah," squawked the parrot as we entered the room. "Go to Jeremiah."

"That's the second time tonight he's said that," I whispered. "Who's Jeremiah?"

"I don't have the slightest idea," said Dolores. "I never heard him say it at all until about four months after the accident. It was as if he learned it after Mother's death—though neither my father nor I taught it to him. For a while, I wondered if it was someone that Mother wanted me to contact. I even looked in her address book. But she didn't know any Jeremiah."

One more bit of weirdness. I was trying to figure out how they all fit together.

We sat on the couch, Dolores between Chris and me. I was on her left side, the side with the scars.

"Now what?" asked Dolores.

"I don't know," I said. "I guess you should try to call your mother."

Dolores closed her eyes. "Mother," she whispered. "Mother, can you hear me?"

Nothing.

"Maybe we should try it," said Chris. "Mrs. Smiley, if you can hear us, come back, come—"

She was interrupted by Commander Cody. "Hello, Sweetie!" he squawked. "Hello, Sweetie!"

Dolores's hand flinched in mine.

For a moment we saw nothing, and I wondered if the bird really was an indicator that the ghost was around. Then Mrs. Smiley shimmered into view, a still-pretty, middle-aged lady whose face was marked by infinite sorrow.

Dolores gasped.

Mrs. Smiley looked at her daughter and shook her head sadly. I felt a surge of relief; at least she wasn't mad.

"Why are you here?" I asked.

No answer. I wasn't surprised. In all the times Chris and I have met ghosts, not one of them has ever spoken to us. It would make life easier if they could.

"Mother," whispered Dolores, "I am so sorry. Can you ever forgive me?"

I wondered if this apology would break whatever tie held the ghost, free her to go on to the next world. But Mrs. Smiley didn't go. Instead, she leaned over to the parrot, as if whispering to him.

"Jeremiah!" it squawked. "Go to Jeremiah!"

The ghost looked at us desperately, as if pleading with us to understand.

That was when I got it. "Was your mother very religious?" I whispered.

Dolores nodded. "Very. It was something else we fought about."

"Don't move. I'll be right back!"

I slipped my hand out of hers, half afraid the ghost would vanish once I did. But she stood in place, a look of desperate hope on her face. I tiptoed up the stairs and into the room Mr. Smiley had assigned to Chris and me.

The family Bible that lay on the dresser was covered with dust. I blew it off, then started to flip through the pages. It took me a moment to find the Book of Jeremiah, but when I did, I struck paydirt. Pressed between the pages were two thin sheets of paper, almost like the stuff you use for airmail. They were so thin you would never have known there was anything in the book if you weren't looking for it.

Glancing at the pages where the letter had been waiting, I saw that two phrases had been underlined in the text. The first was in chapter 31, verse 22: "How long wilt thou go about, O thou backsliding daughter?"

Yow, I thought. *That sure puts a finger on what Mrs. Smiley was all wound up about.*

But the second phrase, which was part of verse 34, gave me hope. It said, "I will forgive their iniquities, and I will remember their sin no more."

I glanced at the letter. The handwriting was wobbly, as if the person who wrote it had been very weak, and it looked unfinished. But I knew Dolores had to see it.

I slipped back down the stairs. When the ghost saw me, saw what I was holding, she burst into tears.

I thrust the letter into Dolores's hand. "Here," I said. "Read this."

She glanced at it. Then, with a quavering voice, she spoke aloud the words her mother had written nearly twenty years earlier, the undelivered letter she had stayed to make sure her daughter finally received.

My Darling Dolores,

As I write these words, we both lie in hospital beds, with little hope that either of us will ever leave them. If the Lord must take one of us, I pray it will be me. You have a whole life ahead of you. I already have too much behind me.

I will have one great sorrow in dying, dear one, which is that I will not be here to see you grow to womanhood. I have, too, one great fear—not of death, for I trust the Lord. My fear is of dying before we can make peace between us.

Oh, my sweet baby girl, how can I say what is in my heart? How can I say how much I love you? You will not know until you are a mother yourself. I would do anything, give anything, to protect you from the sorrow and pain that have come to you. I am so sorry, my beloved. *More* than sorry.

There is one thing you must know if I should die before you wake. *I forgive you.* For whatever part you feel you played in this tragedy, I forgive you. For whatever you fear I am angry about, I forgive you. For whatever sorrow you think you have caused me, I forgive you. For whatever wrong you believe you have done me, I forgive you—as I hope that God and you will forgive me.

Terrible things happen between mothers and daughters, my dear one, but there is a ferocious love that binds us. With all the love I have, I release you from guilt.

Do you remember when you were little and we used to read "The Hunting of the Snark"? The cook said, "I tell you once, I tell you twice, what I tell you three times is true." You used to say that whenever you wanted to convince me of something. Now I tell you once, twice, three times: I forgive you, I forgive you, I forgive you.

That was as far as Mrs. Smiley had written. She must have tucked the letter into the Bible, then died before she could finish it. As her daughter read it aloud now, Mrs. Smiley's ghost drifted toward us. Kneeling before Dolores, she gazed at her with the most radiant look of love I have ever seen.

Something twisted inside me as I wondered where my own mother had gone.

After a moment Mrs. Smiley reached her hand toward Dolores's face. She couldn't touch her, of course. That's the thing with ghosts—

their forms are less than mist, and no matter how they try, they just can't touch you. So Dolores didn't realize her mother was there until she put down the letter and looked up.

Tears streaming down her cheeks, running through the valleys of her scars, she whispered, "Oh, Mother, I miss you, I miss you, I miss you."

Mrs. Smiley nodded in understanding. Yet she seemed sad, as well. She looked up. An expression of great longing crossed her pale and glowing face.

"You have to let go of her, Dolores," I whispered. "She didn't stay all these years because she was angry. She stayed because you needed to know she loved you, needed to know she forgave you. *She stayed because you hadn't let go of her.*"

"Nine's right," said Chris. "You have to let her move on now."

I could see Dolores swallow. "I love you, Mother," she whispered. "I miss you. And . . . I release you."

She said it three times.

I thought it was over. But from the darkness, from a place beyond understanding, another visitor arrived; a young man, pale and transparent, yet quite handsome.

"Bud!" whispered Dolores.

The new ghost smiled at Dolores sadly. Then he floated toward us, bent, and pressed his lips against her scarred cheek. He could not really touch her either, of course. But Dolores knew what he was telling her.

Raising her trembling fingers to her face, she watched as Bud took her mother's hand. He began to lead Mrs. Smiley away from us—out of this world with its sorrows and rages and tragedies, on to a place of perfect forgiveness.

Mrs. Smiley stopped and turned to blow her daughter one last kiss. Then she smiled, turned again, and vanished slowly into the darkness.

Some things don't change, even after you're dead.

THE GROUNDING OF THERESA

Mary Downing Hahn

The first thing I noticed about him wasn't his height or the color of his hair or even his clumsiness. It was the sound of his basketball shoes hitting the asphalt—*thud, thud, thud.* The noise was loud enough to wake the dead.

Then there was his shadow, so much faster than he was, darting here and there, shortening and lengthening, fading and darkening as he moved in and out of the light. For several minutes I leaned against the wall and watched his futile attempts to get the ball through the hoop clean and neat.

When I couldn't stand it any longer, I cleared my throat to let him know he wasn't alone on the court. I must have startled him because he whirled around so fast he dropped the ball. It bounced toward me and I picked it up, loving the pebbly feel of it in my hands. It had been a long

time since I'd played, but I hadn't forgotten. Dribbling close and tight, I ran toward him, leaped, and shot. The ball swished through the hoop without touching the rim.

The boy caught it on the rebound. "Nice shot," he said.

"Thanks." We stared at each other for a moment, two strangers on the school basketball court, his face lit by the white glare of an arc light, mine hidden in the shadow of my baseball cap. Without saying a word, we started to play.

I gave him a real workout, feinting, blocking, stealing the ball, making one perfect shot after another. The August night was hot, muggy, hazy with air pollution. It bothered him a lot more than it did me. In no time he was breathing hard and soaked with sweat—hair, T-shirt, shorts, everything was wet. Too tired to concentrate, he made a wild throw. When the ball missed the backboard, he sat down on the asphalt and watched it bounce away into the darkness.

"That's it for me," he muttered.

Even though he should have retrieved the ball, I ran after it, dribbled across the court, and shot one more perfect basket.

The ball rolled to his feet, but he didn't get up. "Don't you ever miss?"

I sat down beside him, breathing in his nice doggy smell, and shrugged. "I'm pretty good."

He scowled. "Pretty conceited, too."

I shrugged again. "I'm just telling the truth. No sense being modest."

He stared at me. I was glad I was sitting just out of the light's range. "How come I've never seen you before?" he asked. "You new in town?"

"I've been here a while." I kept my answer vague on purpose, hoping to discourage more questions, but my ploy didn't work. He wanted to know how long I was staying, where I was from, what my parents did, all sorts of stuff that was none of his business. The only thing I told him was my name, T. J. Jones. He said his was Jeremy Mason, he was twelve years old, he lived at the end of Adams Street. He was starting eighth grade in the fall and he wanted to go out for basketball.

"The trouble is, I'm short for my age. Most of the guys are taller than I am. It gives them a certain advantage, you know what I mean? So I practice every night. Tryouts aren't till next month, so I figure I might get good enough if I really work at it."

"It's not just your height, Jeremy. Look at me. I'm short, too, but I can play circles around you."

My honesty earned me another scowl. To soften my words, I added, "It's not your fault. Some people have a special gift. They're naturally good at things. Maybe there's something you can do that I'm lousy at. Singing, maybe, or art—I can't carry a tune or draw a straight line."

"It so happens I'm the best artist in my grade." Jeremy was just as immodest as I'd been.

"There you go," I said. "You should practice drawing and forget basketball."

"I'm not interested in being an artist, I want to be a basketball player. I want people to cheer for me. I want them to get up on their feet and shout my name—'Go, Jeremy, go!' "

I cocked my head and listened to the echo bounce off the school wall. It sounded like a whole crowd out there, cheering him on. He heard it, too. I knew he saw himself running down the court, doing a perfect layup, winning the state championship for his school. Hadn't I once had the same dream? Too excited to think my idea through, I said, "How about meeting me here every night? We'll play one-on-one. I'll teach you every trick I know."

For the first time Jeremy smiled. "You'd do that, T.J.?"

"On one condition." I stared deep into his eyes. "Don't ask me any more questions. Don't follow me, don't tell a single soul about me. It has to be a secret. If you bring some other kid with you, you'll never see me again. I swear it."

"Why?" Jeremy was puzzled, maybe even a little scared. I have that effect on people. I'm too intense, I guess, and it makes them nervous.

"It's none of your business why." This time I didn't care whether I offended him or not. It was important to take me seriously. "Promise. Cross your heart and hope to die."

Slowly Jeremy put his hand on his chest.
"Cross my heart," he whispered, "and hope to
die if I ever tell a lie."

"Good." I got to my feet and stared down at
him. "One other thing—we have to meet later.
Someone could come along and see us." I was
finally thinking straight. I'd been so happy to get
my hands on a basketball, I'd forgotten the rules.
It was lucky I hadn't been caught.

Now Jeremy was really worried. "But I have
a curfew." He glanced at his watch. "It's almost
ten o'clock, and I was supposed to be home at
nine-thirty. My parents are probably looking for
me right this minute."

"Midnight," I told him, stepping deeper into
the shadows, "or not at all."

"I'll have to sneak out," Jeremy said. "I could
get in big trouble, T.J."

"Take it or leave it." I was backing away,
keeping my eye on an approaching car, coming
slow, its headlights pointed toward us, threatening to sweep across me.

The driver honked. Jeremy turned to me, but
I was already out of sight. "T.J.!" he yelled.

I didn't answer. From behind a tree I watched
Jeremy walk slowly to the car. His father was
angry. I could hear him yelling and Jeremy apolo-
gizing. Then the car drove away, its headlights
illuminating the empty playground. Without Jeremy the night seemed very quiet. In the distance
traffic rumbled on the interstate, a lonely sound

reminding me of people with places to go and homes to return to.

Home. I had a home, too—only I wasn't happy there.

The next night, long before midnight, I was under my tree, invisible in its shadow, watching and listening for Jeremy. Soon I heard him thudding across the asphalt, bouncing the ball as he ran. "T.J.," he called. "Where are you, T.J.?"

I loved the way his voice echoed, the way his shadow danced with him. "Here I am!" I cried.

Jeremy whirled around, searching for me. I was right behind him, staying in his shadow, laughing. When he saw me, he sucked in his breath, amazed I was so close. "Where did you come from?"

Instead of answering, I grabbed the ball and darted across the court. He followed me, leaping to catch it on the rebound. We played till he collapsed on the asphalt, out of breath, sweaty, exhausted.

"I don't know how you do it," he said, his voice ragged.

Like before, I sat in the shadow. "I rest in the daytime," I told him.

"Me, too, but I can't keep up with you."

I changed the subject then and got him to talk about his family. I wanted to hear all the details. His house, his bedroom, his brother and sister, his mother and father, his dog, what they ate for dinner, did they send out for pizza sometimes, did they go to the ocean or the mountains. I devoured everything he told me, especially the stories about his Irish setter. Next to basketball, the thing I missed most was my dog.

"But what about you, T.J.?" Jeremy asked. "What's your family like?"

That was the biggest danger of asking people too many questions. Sooner or later they wanted to hear about you. I scowled at him, but I had my answer ready. "We made a bargain. No questions—remember?"

He mumbled an apology. "I forgot."

Getting to my feet, I said, "You'd better go home before somebody discovers you aren't in your bed."

"You'll be here tomorrow night?"

"At midnight."

I watched him race his shadow across the court. When he was out of sight but not out of hearing, I followed him down the dark streets, past houses sleeping on moonlit lawns, past cars reflecting streetlights in their windows, past cats gliding from bush to bush on feet as silent as mine. Crouched behind a tree, I saw Jeremy tiptoe up a driveway and let himself into a small brick rambler. He was home safe.

But not alone. I slipped through the door behind him. The house was just as he'd described it, and I went from room to room, touching the things he'd told me about. Patty, the dog, raised her head and stared at me, but she didn't bark.

A cat might arch its back and puff its tail and dance away sideways, but not a dog. They know I mean no harm.

Before I left, I went to Jeremy's room and watched him sleep for a few minutes. I also peeked in on his little sister, Wendy, his brother, Dan, his mother, and his father. I watched TV; I opened the refrigerator and admired all the food, touched it and smelled it, but didn't eat any. It was so much fun I wished I could stay longer, but I knew the rules.

From then on, Jeremy and I played basketball every night. Sometimes I followed him home, sometimes I went to other houses, sometimes I just roamed the streets. Depending on my mood, I climbed trees, borrowed bikes or skateboards, or swam in the community pool, gliding through the still water like a moonbeam. Every now and then Patty came with me. I liked the sound of her paws on the cement, the feel of her warm breath on my hand.

As August slid into September, the nights cooled off. The crisp air smelled like dead leaves instead of honeysuckle. Jeremy began to improve, but just as he was becoming a real challenge, something happened that ruined everything. We were sitting on the asphalt, taking a break. High above, the moon's full face peered down, no bigger than a dime but shining bright, casting more light than I realized.

Jeremy turned to me to say something and sucked in his breath. "T.J., you're, you're . . ." he whispered. "I can't believe I never noticed."

I backed away, too shocked to say a word. Jeremy had always struck me as the most unobservant boy I'd ever met. Now he was on to me, he'd discovered my true nature, and I was in big trouble.

He laughed at my behavior. "It's okay, T.J. I don't mind playing basketball with a girl. I'm just surprised it took me so long to realize, that's all."

Limp with relief, I let my breath out in a long sigh. "Of course I'm a girl. I thought you knew."

Jeremy shook his head. "Do I feel dumb! It never occurred to me a girl could be named T.J. or play basketball like a pro. Plus it's always dark when we meet. I haven't had a chance to get a good look at you."

Moving closer, he reached for my baseball cap. "Take that off so I can see your face."

"No." I was on my feet, running across the dark playground, leaping the wall that separated it from my home. The lawn was freshly mown. The gardener must have cut it while I was asleep. It smelled warm and sweet, the essence of last summer's sunshine.

"Wait, T.J.!" Jeremy yelled. "Don't go!"

I glanced back. He'd jumped the wall, too. He was coming after me, shouting, pounding the ground with his heavy feet, breathing hard, making noise, so much noise, more than enough to wake the dead.

"I told you not to follow me!" I turned away from him and saw my parents waiting for me, their faces stern and pale.

"Dearly beloved daughter Theresa," Mom said sadly. "It appears you've broken the rules again."

"You'll be grounded fifty years for this," Dad said. "Perhaps you'll remember the rules the next time we let you out to play."

Aching with pain in the cold place that used to be my heart, I looked at Jeremy. He was standing still, frozen with fear, as rigid as the angel on the pedestal behind him. I took off my cap and showed him my face. It was a spiteful thing to do, but I was angry. Because of him I would not see the stars or the moon for fifty long years. Watching him turn and run, I laughed. His scream was the last sound I'd hear till my punishment was over.

"Come, beloved daughter." Dad took my arm, and slowly, silently, like autumn leaves drifting down from trees, we laid ourselves to rest.

*I have known Jim Macdonald for nearly fifteen
years and would trust him with my life.
He has sworn to me that every word of the
following is true. I believe him.*

A TRUE STORY

James D. Macdonald

This is going to be one of the more unusual stories in this book, because it's true, every word.
It really happened to me.

We'd moved into our house about four years
before. My mother was out somewhere with my
sister and brother; my father was at work. I was
in the dining room doing my homework, at
maybe three-thirty on a spring afternoon. The
sun was shining; there wasn't a storm blowing
up or anything like that.

I was sitting in a big easy chair when I
looked up from my book and saw something
coming out of the kitchen, a dozen feet in front
of me. It was a tall patch of misty light, about the
size and shape of an adult human, but indistinct.

I couldn't make out a face, or even arms or legs, but I knew right away what it was. It was a ghost. It scared me.

The ghost moved through the room toward me with a gliding motion at easy walking speed. A couple of feet in front of where I was sitting it made a turn and went through the doorway to my right, where the front hall, the front door, and the stairway to the second floor were located. It went out of sight around the corner.

I've always been sure that it was a ghost. There's no way that I might have been asleep and dreaming, or coming down with something. It was real.

Like lots of true stories, this story doesn't have a neat wrap-up. No buried treasure in the yard, no secret room with a skeleton locked inside, no old newspaper clippings telling of a tragic death in the house a long time before.

I've been a lot of places since then, and seen a lot of things, but never anything like that.

So that's my story of what I saw one day, and like I said, it's true. Make of it what you will.

When King Arthur was a boy, before it was known that he would be king, he lived with a foster father named Sir Ector, and a foster brother named Cai (sometimes written as Kay). Here is an adventure Arthur and Cai might have had in the spirit-haunted forests of Olde England.

THE POOKA

Michael Markiewicz

Father's longbow was much larger than mine, and I was having difficulty stringing it. I braced the shiny weapon between my legs and pulled. The powerful wooden spring twisted around my thigh as I struggled to get the cord into the notch. Just as it was about to slip into place, however, I began to lose my grip. I desperately fought to control the mighty bow, but it was no use.

My little brother, Arthur, did nothing to help. Arthur was busy sharpening our father's arrows and didn't even notice my predicament. Without warning, the bow spun around and the string snapped on backward.

I jumped into the air, startling Trossee, our

father's warhorse, and began hopping around the open stable, bellowing a strange tune. Most verses went something like "OWWWGETTHIS— OWWOFFME—OWWWMYLEG!"

Arthur didn't seem impressed. Then I started a whirling dancelike step, which seemed to get his attention. Actually it was when the bow whacked him on the back of the head that he jumped to his feet and joined my show.

"OWMYHEAD," he wailed.

"OWMYLEG," I replied.

"OWJERK!"

"OWSTUPID!"

"OWWWWWWWWWW!"

"QUIET!" screamed a voice from the castle's parapet above. It was our father, Lord Ector, and he did not seem pleased. "You two will never get those arrows ready for tomorrow's battle at this rate," he snorted.

The war in the south lay heavy on Father's mind. He had brought us to Lord Rapart's castle to help prepare for a battle near the Harwary Run and probably thought my situation was of little concern. I didn't agree, but I wasn't about to argue with him, especially since he had told us not to even touch his bow. Also, he had warned us that if we got in the way or caused trouble, he would tell one of the wisewomen to conjure up the Pooka and have us spirited away.

That was a dire threat. The mysterious legend of the Pooka kept most people out of Lord

Rapart's woods. The story told of a ghostly horse that roamed the forests at twilight, dragging a long chain from its neck and terrifying anyone who saw it. People said the Pooka could wrap its heavy chain around you and steal your soul forever.

"Sorry, my lord," I yelped as Arthur wrenched the bow from my leg.

"Sorry won't help tomorrow if that bow is broken, Cai," Father replied roughly. "Since you two have time to play the fool, you can take Trossee down to the smithy and have his hooves cleaned. And then finish those arrows!"

"But it's getting dark," I answered. "What if the Pooka—"

"Move or I'll come down there!"

"We're going, we're going!" we shouted.

Arguing with Father was like trying to reason with a wild boar. Even our family crest was a boar on a red field. Father had said it symbolized our strength, but I think it was really a comment about our family's pigheadedness.

We unhitched the horse and set off through a narrow wooded path that led to the smith's hovel. As we lost sight of the castle in the tangled branches behind us, I suddenly had a brilliant idea.

"Say," I schemed, "why don't we just find a stream around here and clean his hooves ourselves? Then we wouldn't have to walk all the way to the smithy."

"We don't have any tools, and besides—"

"Look, we get Trossee in the stream, the water loosens the clods in his hooves, and we scrape them out with some rocks or something."

"I don't know, Cai."

"You want to walk back through these woods after dark and get grabbed by the Pooka?"

"Where's there a stream?" Arthur asked furtively.

"That's the spirit," I replied.

We walked down a grassy slope and left the path in search of a stream. Through a ravine and across several small meadows we finally saw the gleam of water in a nearby valley. We dashed for it and made fast work of Trossee's hooves.

It would have gone faster, but the big horse kept losing his balance on the slippery moss-covered rocks. He nearly stepped on my foot twice. Luckily he stepped on Arthur's instead. We'd have finished much earlier except that Arthur kept hopping around shouting curses at the dumb animal, and I wound up doing most of the scraping.

I didn't do a very good job, but I wanted to get back to the castle right away. I just hoped that Father wouldn't notice the sloppy workmanship. As soon as I had chipped off the large chunks, we went in search of the path. Unfortunately, as the sun dropped behind the western sky, I began to have a sinking feeling in my stomach. We were becoming hopelessly lost in the long shadows and darkening silhouettes. After a bit we came upon a small knoll where I mounted Trossee and tried to find the tower of Rapart's keep.

"Can you see the castle?" asked Arthur nervously.

"No."

"Can you see the path we were on?"

"No."

"Well, what do you see?"

"I see that we're really lost in a haunted forest in the dark."

"I hate you," said my terrified little brother.

We moved on to another hill and then another until we were deep within a thick, foreboding stand of trees.

"Cai?" said Arthur, breaking the still night air. "Do you suppose these woods are *really* haunted?"

"No. People just say that to keep strangers out of here," I answered as we plodded along aimlessly. I said it with such conviction I almost believed it myself, but as I listened to the noises in the wood, I was convinced that I was dead wrong.

We were scrambling up another rocky embankment, just above a misty thicket of trees, when we saw something move in the distance. A strange white shape crept out of the blackness and froze us with fear. Then we heard a jangling chain and a cry like a wild animal in torment. It could only be one thing: the Pooka!

Trossee whinnied and bucked frantically. He kicked and pulled his reins as the ghost horse called from the darkness of the forest. Then our father's best steed snapped his leather stays and charged into the woods. Arthur and I ran after him, but it was useless. Mesmerized by the Pooka, our mount quickly disappeared into the night with the specter close behind him.

Now we were in real trouble. It would have been better if the Pooka had taken us instead. We had lost our father's favorite horse just before an important battle. He'd be furious, and some of the knights might even think we were traitors. There was only one thing to do.

"Cai?" said my little brother with a tremble.

"Mmm?"

"I'm not going out into those woods to look for that stupid horse."

"Okay," I replied. "Then stay here and get caught by the Pooka, or, when you get back home, go and tell Father how we lost Trossee."

Arthur paused and then started toward the trees.

At first we could follow Trossee's hoofprints, but as we continued, they became harder to find in the thick undergrowth. We went on for what seemed like miles until we finally lost the trail completely in a small glade between a bog and another stream.

"If he ran up this stream, we'll lose his prints in the water," I said as I peered into the murky blackness.

"And if he went through those bogs down there, we'll never find him," responded Arthur.

We desperately searched for some trace of the animal, but there was none. The last print was so faint it was hardly noticeable, and the moonlight was fading fast. Trossee could have gone in almost any direction from here.

Then, once more, we heard the unmistakable cry of the Pooka. The soft wail quickly grew to a shrieking howl as something bolted from the brush only thirty yards away. A ghostly steed rumbled out of the forest like a tempest with hooves. It snapped its lips and reared up on its hind legs—beautiful and terrifying at the same time. For a second it just stared at us with its fiery eyes. It seemed almost intelligent, as though it were sizing us up. Then it whirled about and tore off into the thick bog in the lower valley.

Arthur was visibly shaken by the whole ordeal, but I was quite calm. In fact, I was so calm that I decided to lie down and take a short nap. Generally, I don't fall face forward into the brush when I sleep, but I guess I was really tired. It all became too much for Arthur, however, and he actually began slapping me in the face and saying my name over and over again. I really think he was losing his mind.

"Cai, I think it wants us to follow it into the bog," Arthur said.

"You go follow it, and I'll stay here in case Trossee comes by," I said groggily.

"I think we should both go after it."

"Well, don't blame me if we miss Trossee," I said, staggering to my feet.

"We'll come back this way and check, after we go and see if the Pooka is down there."

"Down *there*?" I replied.

"In the bog," explained Arthur.

"In the bog?" I asked.

"Yes, in the—"

"If I were you boys, I wouldn't go into the bog!" shouted an ominous voice out of the dark.

I turned defiantly to the intruder and said, "Hold, stranger, or I'll run you through." Actually, that's what I meant to say. It came out more like "AHHHHH!"

I figured my war cry would scare him away. Arthur appeared to agree with this tactic. We actually screamed quite well, but it seemed to scare us more than it did the dark shrouded figure.

From behind one of the bushes emerged a small bearded man with a well-worn cloak and a face to match. He had deep-set eyes and a smile that cut across his cheeks like a wide valley. He seemed friendly, but there was something strange about him.

"Didn't mean to frighten you boys, but I wouldn't advise following the Pooka into the bog. She's a nasty one and might catch you in there," he warned as he eyed the family crest on my tunic.

"Oh . . . thanks," I replied, confused and just a bit terrified.

"I'm sorry for scaring you," he continued. "My name is Beal, Squire Beal, and you are . . . ?"

"I'm Cai," I answered, "and this is my brother, Arthur. We're looking for our father's horse."

"Ah! The steed I saw just a while ago with the boar's crest and a broken rein."

"That's him!" cried Arthur. "Where is he?"

"Hmm . . . I suppose I could just lead you to him, but maybe you could help me first," he said with a gleam.

"Yes?" I asked.

"I've got a proposition for you. They say that after the moon sets, the spirits become whole. According to the legend, if you can ride the Pooka when it is in this form and unfasten its chain, it will become tame. I can take you to a spot where I could jump on its back and—"

"Why do you need us?" I asked. "Why don't you just ride it yourself?"

"Hmm . . . I'm not fond of the idea of getting caught by it and dragged off to the netherworld, I suppose. So, I need someone to take off the chain while I ride it. . . . I'm sure we could catch it easily."

"And if we manage to tame it?" Arthur asked.

"Then I'll gladly take you to your steed."

"*If* we manage to tame it?!" I shouted at Arthur. "Are you insane? What if we *don't* manage to tame it?"

"Then we'll be kept forever in the lower realms as the Pooka's prisoners," answered the squire flatly.

This was not a good choice: get captured by some raging spectral horse or explain to our father how we lost his most-prized mount.

"We'll do it," Arthur said.

"We will?" I argued.

"*You* want to explain how a Pooka got Trossee?"

"We'll do it," I replied.

Beal took us to a valley where he said the Pooka had been seen several times. He was sure that if we waited for a bit, the ghostly horse would appear. We climbed a large oak and positioned ourselves on a sturdy branch. After what seemed like hours, we were about to give up when we heard the familiar wail again.

We watched in terror as the glowing specter drew near. Closer and closer it trotted toward us until it was nearly straight below.

"Now!" yelled Beal as he lunged for the beast.

Arthur and I dived for the huge neck while the squire landed neatly on the thing's back.

The creature let out a scream like nothing I had ever heard. It jumped into the air and flailed its legs wildly as Arthur grasped the heavy coils of chain. He held one end as the beast bucked and threw itself into the trees.

The chain was flying around like a whip of steel. The one end nearly caught my head, but I ducked just in time. I grabbed one of the deadly links and held on for dear life as the specter tossed me into the air. Arthur had managed to get one of the coils off its neck but was now struggling just to hold on.

"I don't think this was such a good idea!" I screamed as the Pooka raked me with its hooves.

"Maybe not!" yelled Arthur.

"Try to get . . . the chain off!" Beal shouted as he fought to keep his seat on the Pooka's back.

Arthur began to slide the whole mass up the monster's neck. Suddenly it reared up again and pinned his arms under the heavy links.

"I'm stuck!" he screamed.

I grabbed the Pooka's snout and pulled down with all my might. At first it didn't budge, but then its eyes fixed upon my crest, and it suddenly weakened. I could hardly believe it when the horse's head bowed down to me. Arthur quickly shoved the chain coils over the ears, and they fell to the ground in a heap.

As the last coil dropped from its neck, the

horse stood bolt upright and came to attention. Its whole appearance changed. The steed's color was now a pale gray, and its eyes seemed gentle and friendly. It even accepted commands from its rider.

"You did it!" shouted Beal joyfully.

"Okay . . . now," I panted. "You've got your horse . . . where's ours?"

"A deal is a deal. Follow me," said the squire with a broad grin.

We followed him into another brush-filled valley. I was somewhat suspicious of the squire's plans until I spied Trossee in a small clearing and noticed Rapart's castle in the distance.

"Well, your lord will be delighted to see this prize," I said as I patted the now solidified ghost and then grabbed Trossee's broken rein.

"My lord will be pleased to get his mount back," Beal replied with an odd grin.

"What do you mean, 'get his mount back'?" I asked.

"I am squire to Falthion," replied the man with a wink.

"Oh, I've heard of him," said Arthur. "He was a great knight who died at the Battle of Larwan. But . . . wait . . . you can't be . . . you'd be over a hundred years old!"

"Maybe I am," said the stranger in a mysterious tone.

I felt the hairs on the back of my neck begin to dance.

"Who are you?" I demanded with a whimper.

"I'm a ghost just like the Pooka," Beal explained. "I was keeping watch the night before the Battle of Larwan. When I fell asleep, some of the enemy came and captured Falthion's favorite horse. The next day my lord was trampled to death by a rider using his steed. His beloved mount was turned against him, and it was my fault for being so lazy. The horse went insane after that and had to be killed. I guess that was why it became a Pooka.

"I was killed when the enemy breached the walls. Only then did I learn of the curse my lord had spoken as he lay dying on the battlefield. He had doomed me to chase after his horse until I could make a wild boar take off its chain. When I saw your crest, I knew the curse could be ended. . . . Thank you."

Arthur and I looked at each other in disbelief. Not only had we seen the Pooka, we had spent the evening in the company of a ghost. I began to feel another nap coming on.

"I must go now," he continued. "Falthion is still waiting for his mount to be returned, and I'm not going to shirk my responsibility again."

With that he mounted the ghost horse. The two rode straight through a tree and disappeared down an old, unused path. Arthur and I stood there for a while, too shaky to move, and then returned to the castle in a daze.

We got back just as the sun was beginning to pierce the low brush. We tied Trossee and flopped down, completely exhausted. Then we saw our father leaving the courtyard.

"You two have been awfully quiet down here all night. Everything all right?" he inquired as he adjusted his armor.

"Yes, fine," we replied weakly. We knew no one would believe that we had actually captured the Pooka, so we had agreed to keep it a secret.

"All the arrows sharpened?" he asked pointedly.

I had completely forgotten about them in all the excitement. It would take hours to finish the job, and I was worn out. We probably could have passed them off as done, but then Arthur spoke up.

"We're still working on them," he answered.

"We are?" I asked as I glared at my little brother.

"Yes, we are!"

"Make sure they're finished soon. We'll need them for the battle," our father instructed.

"We'll get them done right away," answered Arthur as our father went back into the courtyard and gathered some of the knights for drills.

"After all we've been through!" I scolded. "No one would know these aren't done!"

"We would have known. . . . Besides, do you want to spend the rest of eternity sharpening arrows?"

I thought of Beal falling asleep at the Battle of Larwan and trying to undo the curse for all those years. I looked at the pile of arrows and realized that, sometimes, Arthur made a lot of sense. After we finished the arrows, I made sure to go over Trossee's hooves—just for good measure.

*Ghosts are not the only things that
haunt a person's soul.*

GHOST WALK

Mark A. Garland

"I hate coming here," Arin said, looking around
with nervous eyes. "It's too scary."

Marianne frowned. "You always say that, but
it's not. Not really. I've been here many times."

"But what if he actually comes tonight?"

Arin's mother grinned like a Halloween
pumpkin. "*That* is what we're counting on,"
she said.

Arin let her shoulders sag. There was no getting out of it; her mother had kept after her until
she finally agreed to visit the little church and
the big graveyard that spread out behind it. She
looked the place over more closely now, the tall
steeple, the long wooden side boards turned
blotchy gray where most of the paint had long
ago fallen off.

A red and white FOR SALE sign was planted in

the tall grass in the front yard. The new church had been built last year, a half mile up the road.

Marianne walked past the front steps, around to the big yard, and Arin followed. Kids had thrown rocks through some of the pretty stained-glass windows, probably the Rayner boys over on Ledge Street. They were always wrecking everything; or maybe it was that big kid Kenny Becker and the little fan club that followed him around all the time.

There weren't any other kids around here tonight, though, and Arin didn't think there would be. The wind had died, the storm had passed, but the ground was still soaked. The air had gotten cold, and thick dark clouds still filled the evening sky. Every kid in town was home, dry and warm, watching the new fall TV shows. Almost every kid.

Just past the side walkway stood the first tombstones.

"I wanna go," Arin said, trying to insist. "He's gonna be here any minute, walking the graves. I'm just not ready to meet up with someone from the other side."

"We have to stay, and you know it. Don't back out now, Arin, please! He was your father, after all. Not even death can change that."

Arin kept walking, one step at a time. The tombstones near the church were the oldest, some from the Civil War, though in the fading light she couldn't read any of them. Her father had shown the graves to her once, shown her how you could figure out the ages of the people from the dates. Nobody lived very long in the old days, it seemed. Sometimes that was still true.

Toward the other end of the graveyard the stones were newer, some only a few months old, or a couple of years.

Arin looked up and froze. "It's him!" she said, then she faded behind Marianne and peeked out around her hips. He was as tall as Arin remembered, taller than Marianne, but he looked darker somehow, and much thinner. His eyes were set too deeply in his tired face, making them almost invisible in the near-darkness. She watched him moving slowly, evenly, across the grass, coming toward her.

"What if he can't hear me?" Arin asked. "What if he doesn't want us here at all? We shouldn't have come!"

But Marianne went forward, leaving Arin no choice but to follow. They all reached the grave at the same time.

Her father turned and faced the gravestone. Arin couldn't see his face well enough, but she could hear the sounds he began to make, a whimpering noise. *He's crying*, Arin thought, which seemed so strange. She had never heard him cry in life.

"He doesn't seem to know we're here," Arin said, but as she did, her father's head turned and

he looked over his shoulder, looked almost right at her. Then he looked away again.

"No," Marianne whispered, "but I think he can hear us, more or less. Maybe not with his ears, but he hears us."

The man who had been Arin's father looked up then and gazed out across the yard, toward the church.

"Go ahead, tell him," Marianne prodded.

"I don't think I can," Arin replied.

Marianne glared at her. "I have tried my best, I've told him how I feel, but it's not enough. Now *you* have to try. You *have* to. He's bound to this place. That's why he comes here night after night. We need to set him free!"

"Okay," Arin agreed, because she knew that it was true.

The man's head turned again. He was barely visible at all now, it had gotten so dark. Arin moved a step closer.

"You don't have to stay around here any-more," she told her father. "You did everything you could have, and more. You always did! I'm grateful for the time we had together, not sad because of what we might have had. We're all right, Daddy. And so are you."

She thought about the night the two men had robbed the little church. Arin had gone with her mother to help her father finish cleaning, which had been his part-time job. The robbers had come in just after that. She remembered screaming as her father tried to throw the men out, then two shots being fired by one man while the other used the butt of his rifle like a club.

The old church hadn't been used since that night.

"Daddy," Arin went on, "you were so brave. You only did what you thought was right, which was what you always did. Nobody can blame you for doing that."

Even as she spoke, the words seemed to have a strange effect on him. Her father turned slowly in a circle, only a dark shape in the night now, but Arin could sense the weight leaving his shoulders, could imagine his spirit glowing more brightly—free, or finally getting there. He was taking a last look, she thought. At least, she hoped he was.

"I love you guys," Arin's father said, speaking to the darkness, thinking out loud, perhaps. His voice was so quiet, Arin thought, as if it almost wasn't there at all.

"We love you, too," Arin and her mother said, both at the same time.

The clouds parted then. Stars appeared, spreading over half the sky, and the moon suddenly shone down on the church and the graveyard, providing enough light to read by. Marianne went to stand before the wide face of the tombstone, stood beside her husband, reading the names. Arin stood for a moment, snuggled in between them, but then her father started to leave.

He walked silently between the other gravestones, slowly at first, then picked up speed, like a big ship heading out to sea. She heard him pull his keys out of his pocket as he neared his car in the parking lot.

"Do you think it worked?" Arin asked.

"Do you?"

Arin nodded. "I think so."

Her mother smiled. Then both of them rose up slowly and drifted into the sky, toward the moon, toward the stars, fading as they went.

Love is not the only thing that can last
beyond the grave. . . .

FOR LOVE OF HIM

Vivian Vande Velde

It was no good trying to outrun the rain. Harrison realized that after those few frantic seconds when the first big drops pelted the leaves in the uppermost branches, hard enough to be audible. Already soaked, he wasn't running, for the roads in the old section of the cemetery could be treacherously slippery. He was caught, naturally, just about halfway between the cemetery office where the rest rooms were and the area where his troop was helping Allan earn his Eagle Badge by cleaning up litter and debris from around the graves.

He almost missed seeing the woman kneeling by a grave not far from the road. It was only the near-simultaneous flash of lightning and crack of thunder that caused him to jerk his head up, into the eye-stinging rain. For a moment he thought he was seeing mist, a product of the combination of hot spring day and cold rain.

As soon as he saw it was a woman in a white dress, Harrison stopped looking, reluctant to intrude on someone's privacy, even if that person was unaware of him.

But then he glanced back.

The woman just knelt there as though oblivious to Harrison, to the pouring rain, to the danger of a thunderstorm with all these centuries-old trees around. She rocked back and forth, her pale hands covering her face. Her white dress and her long dark hair were plastered to her body, giving her the look of a black-and-white photograph. Even from the road, Harrison could see her shoulders shaking.

Strange, he thought, that anybody should be so overcome by grief here in the old part of the cemetery. Most of these graves dated back to the 1800's. That was why this section looked so like a park: The Victorians had had a weird perspective on things. These days sightseers came here to take pictures of the grand angels, or to make rubbings of the stones with their elaborate carvings and their flowery testimonials.

Why such heartfelt tears for someone dead at least a hundred years?

Harrison glimpsed Mr. Reisinger's van rounding the hill on the lower road. "Mr. R.!" he called, waving his arms, though with the rain and thunder and distance the Scoutmaster couldn't possibly hear.

But he must have been on the lookout for Harrison. He flashed his headlights to show he'd spotted him.

Harrison watched the van make its way around the pond before he remembered the woman. Should he offer her a ride? But the woman was no longer there. Silly, Harrison thought. You'd think she'd come to the road on a day like this, rather than cut across the back way to the old buggy path. But perhaps she'd been embarrassed to have been caught at . . . whatever.

Harrison stepped onto the rain-slicked grass. "Miss?" he called over the surly rumbling of thunder. The sheet of rain prevented him from seeing far at all. He thought he caught a glimpse of a figure beyond the willow tree, but that seemed to be a man, a tall, thin, dark-haired man. And then he was gone, too.

"Miss?"

Harrison took another step. He heard the crunch of gravel as the van came up on the road behind him. "Do you want a ride?" he called. "You shouldn't be out here during a lightning storm."

There was no answer, but by then Harrison was almost to the grave by which the woman had been kneeling. He took the few extra steps.

It was a double headstone. ROBERT DELANO ADAMS was inscribed on one side.

LOVING SON
LONG WILL HE BE REMEMBERED
LONG WILL HE BE MISSED

HIS MOTHER GRIEVES STILL

JANUARY 10, 1874–MAY 17, 1892

A hundred years ago today. What an odd coincidence. He did the mental arithmetic. Only a few years older than himself. The other side bore the name EULALIA MEINYK. There was only one date, two days later than the other: MAY 19, 1892.

SHE DIED FOR LOVE OF HIM

How very sad, Harrison thought.

Mr. Reisinger beeped the horn, calling him back to here and now, and motioned for him to get moving.

He clambered in next to Spense, who made a face at Harrison for dripping on him.

"Don't know enough to come in out of the rain," Mr. Reisinger said over the noise of the windshield wipers. He shook his head, but reached under the seat and pulled out a roll of paper towels, which he passed back.

"We get enough done?" Harrison asked.

Mr. Reisinger was a professional gardener who had contracts to take care of several dozen of the newer graves, so he'd be very fussy about the cleanup the Scouts had done. But he said, "Probably," and Harrison leaned back in his seat.

"You smell like a wet dog," Spense complained, friendly as always.

Harrison gazed out the window as they approached the stone and iron gate. How pretty the trees looked, their leaves still fresh and new, the trunks and branches stained dark by the rain, with the dramatically gray clouds as backdrop. Robert Delano Adams and Eulalia Meinyk. He wondered which one the woman had been crying for.

The next day, Monday, Harrison was riding his bike home from school and decided to cut through the cemetery.

We did a good job, he told himself, but then he rounded a corner and saw that somebody had lopped the heads off all the tulips Mr. Reisinger had planted over Mrs. Reisinger's grave. In fact, for the entire length of this row, wreaths were knocked off their stands, ivy and geraniums were trampled. When Harrison got off the bike and walked around to the other side, he saw that someone had used a red felt-tip marker to deface the fronts of the headstones. A few had obscene messages scrawled on them, but many simply had a line drawn through the names, as though the vandals had just held the marker out as they strolled past.

Stupid, senseless malice. And this was just the kind of thing Mr. Reisinger had complained the police were useless for. They'd take the report—they always took a report—but they weren't interested unless there was dramatic breakage. Angrily, Harrison got out the linen handkerchief his mother always tucked into his backpack and spat on it. On his knees he scrubbed at Mrs. Reisinger's headstone—one of the ones that was simply scribbled on. It was bad enough. The ink came off the smooth surface fairly easily, but he had to scrape it out of the engraved areas of the letters.

Finished, he sat back on his heels. On the grave to the left, someone had covered the inscription MOTHER with a particularly crude word. The grave was not one of the ones Mr. Reisinger was responsible for, but it was a recent grave and had been well tended. But now the urn with fresh flowers had been overturned. Harrison could just picture this poor woman's husband and children coming with some new flowers this weekend and seeing that obscenity. With a sigh he began scrubbing at the word.

Three hours later he'd scrubbed clean all the gravestones with actual words on them. The knees of his school pants were filthy, and his hands were too sore to do any more. *Sorry*, he thought to the others.

The scents of crushed flowers and damp earth heated by the sun mingled and hung heavily about him. What was the matter with him, he thought, taking on other people's responsibilities? He'd just spent all afternoon cleaning gravestones for people he didn't even know, who wouldn't even be aware of what he'd done, who might not even care. And for what? He was late for dinner, which always made his mother crazy, he'd missed the chance to go to the library to research his science paper, which was due tomorrow, and he still had to pick up a snack for the Scout meeting tonight.

Harrison jammed what was left of the handkerchief into his pocket, unsure whether he was more sad or angry.

Somehow, despite all the times he had been here, he missed the turnoff to the exit. He was pedaling past the reconstructed Victorian gazebo before he realized he was in the old section. Rather than backtrack, he kept going. The road circled around anyway and came out near the old chapel. There was the grave of abolitionist Frederick Douglass. On the other side of that hill were buried the poor nameless children who had died in the turn-of-the-century orphanage fire. Over there just beyond the curve of the road was the infant son of Wild West showman Buffalo Bill Cody. Instead of going that way, Harrison turned down the road to bring him deeper into the cemetery. He slowed down, unsure he'd recognize it, sure he must have passed it already. Then—just as he was about to give up—he spotted it. Robert Delano Adams. Eulalia Meinyk.

He left the bike by the road.

What am I doing here? he asked himself. Surely he hadn't expected the strange dark-haired woman to still be here.

He ran his fingers across the cool marble, tracing the outlines of the letters. ROBERT DELANO ADAMS. EULALIA MEINYK. SHE DIED FOR LOVE OF HIM.

Two days later. Had she died of a broken heart? People used to do that, back then. What must he have been like for her to be unable to go on without him? Had she taken her own life? SHE DIED FOR LOVE OF HIM.

Without planning it, Harrison sat down next to the grave. *What am I doing here?* he asked himself again.

Just resting, he answered himself. *As soon as I catch my breath, I'll be on my way.*

But the next thing he knew, it was dark out, and Mr. Reisinger was shaking his shoulder.

"What?" he said. "What is it?"

"What is it?" the Scoutmaster repeated. "It's nine o'clock at night, and your parents are frantic. The whole troop and half the neighborhood are out looking for you. What are you doing?"

"I must have fallen asleep," Harrison said. But he was still sitting up, and he knew his eyes had been wide open, though he couldn't remember what he'd been looking at.

The groundskeeper who'd opened the gate for Mr. Reisinger told Harrison to keep out of the cemetery from now on, his parents told him to keep out of the cemetery, the police told him to keep out of the cemetery.

But his science teacher made him stay after school because his report wasn't done, and he didn't want to worry his parents being late again, so he took the shortcut anyway.

Everything's fine, he told himself, ignoring the pounding of his heart and the damp feeling around the edge of his scalp. So why were his hands slippery on the handlebars?

He rode past the stone chapel and into the old section, where the trees were tall and the roads wound dizzyingly, and the graves seemed scattered randomly in the most improbable places rather than being lined up in neat rows. He was aware that he was breathing with his mouth open, and still he couldn't get enough air. What was the matter with him?

He stopped pedaling and the bike coasted to a stop. For several minutes he just sat there straddling his bike, staring straight ahead.

A woman and her dog jogged by, the dog's chain collar jangling.

Harrison finally turned his head and faced the double headstone. ROBERT DELANO ADAMS. MAY 17, 1892. EULALIA MEINYK. MAY 19, 1892. SHE DIED FOR LOVE OF HIM. Harrison closed his eyes. SHE DIED FOR LOVE OF HIM.

He left the bike and approached the gravesite. 1874–1892. Robert had been eighteen when he'd died. Of what? And how old had Eulalia been? SHE DIED FOR LOVE OF HIM. A hundred years ago today. Had they been engaged? Was that why they were buried together? If so, she was probably a little bit younger than him. Maybe about Harrison's age, since people back then married young. Harrison had lived near the cemetery for as long as he could remember, but he had never thought about dying before, about being dead.

He thought about it now.

He put his hand on the stone and tried to imagine what Robert and Eulalia had been like. It was they who had been here Sunday afternoon, he was sure of it. He had seen pictures of people of the late 1800's skating on the Genesee River, the men in top hats, the women with fur muffs. He imagined Robert and Eulalia skating on the river. Had they come to the cemetery for Sunday picnics, the way the cemetery tour guides said Victorians used to do, sitting perhaps on that hill there, overlooking the pond? Harrison imagined them laughing together, their voices clear as angels' song, so much in love that one couldn't live without the other. ROBERT DELANO ADAMS. EULALIA MEINYK. SHE DIED FOR LOVE OF HIM. Nobody loved Harrison that much. Nobody ever would.

"Kid?" the breeze seemed to whisper. "Kid?" Then, more insistant, more human, "Are you all right?"

Harrison opened his eyes and found that he had somehow ended up kneeling on the ground. He blinked in the bright sunlight. Birds were chirping. In the distance, at the farthest edge of hearing, someone was mowing a lawn. The woman jogger with the dog stood poised on the grass between him and the curb as though unsure how close she should approach. She held on to the dog's collar to keep him from bounding over to Harrison.

"I'm"—his voice sounded so husky and unused—"taking a shortcut home so I won't be late." He ran his tongue over his parched lips.

The jogger hesitated before nodding. "Oh." Her jaw twitched, perhaps an attempt at a smile. She took a step back toward the road.

Harrison pulled himself up by leaning on the gravestone.

The jogger tugged on the chain collar until she and her dog were both on the road. Harrison checked his bicycle's wheels and chain and handlebars and seat while the two of them disappeared over the crest of the hill. Then he got back off and knelt by the grave.

SHE DIED FOR LOVE OF HIM. Harrison didn't think he could bear the incredible sadness of it. That they had lived and loved and died before he had even been born. Before his parents had been born. History had always seemed unreal to him— as though everything that had ever happened in the whole of the world had been leading up to him, to whatever moment he was experiencing. Now he felt unreal. Surely things had peaked here, in 1892, for Robert and Eulalia. Surely he was superfluous, extra, unneeded. Not smart. Not loved. Worthless. Nobody would ever grieve at his grave.

We would, a voice whispered into his ear, a voice as warm and beautiful and clear as the singing of angels. *We'd have enough love left over for you. Come to us. Trust us.*

Harrison lay down on the grave and closed his eyes.

We're the ones who care for you, another gentle voice whispered. *Only we. No one else.*

But then a shadow fell across him, blocking out the sun so that he shivered. "Hello, Harrison," a quiet voice said.

Harrison looked up and blinked several times to get the tears out of his eyes. Tears for himself. Tears for Robert and Eulalia. They were waiting for him. They'd make everything better.

"Remember me? Charlie Sonneman?"

SHE DIED FOR LOVE OF HIM. Slowly the vision retreated; the voices retreated. That was all right. He'd be able to call them back. "Hello, Mr. Sonneman," he said. This was Mr. Reisinger's partner in the gardening business. Or at least he had been. Vaguely Harrison remembered hearing that Mr. Sonneman had retired last summer for health reasons. Why was he bothering Harrison now?

"How are you doing, Harrison?"

"Fine," Harrison said, still lying flat on his back.

"I was wondering if you could give me a lift to the gatehouse."

Harrison would have thought Mr. Sonneman was too old for riding double on a bike, but apparently Mr. Sonneman didn't think so. He was annoyed at the interruption, but he figured he could always come back.

"Hasn't your father ever told you," Mr.

Sonneman asked as he took hold of the edge of the seat behind Harrison, "not to talk to strangers?"

"You're not a stranger, Mr. Sonneman."

"I'm not talking about me. I'm talking about those two: Robert Adams and Eulalia Meinyk."

Harrison slammed on the brakes hard enough to jerk them both forward.

"Probably you should go home for the rest of the day," Mr. Sonneman said, ignoring the sudden stop, ignoring the expression that must have been on Harrison's face as Harrison turned to stare at him. "Tomorrow will be easier. You'll be out of danger then. Anniversaries are a powerful thing. As are thunderstorms. And hate."

"She died for love of him," Harrison protested.

Mr. Sonneman shrugged. "Robert's mother wrote that. She never would believe anything bad about him. But Eulalia knew. He was a drunk and a cheat. He used to beat her. Eulalia got hold of a revolver, one of those little white-painted, very ladylike jobs they used to make, and blew his head off."

"That can't be true," Harrison protested.

Mr. Sonneman continued as though Harrison hadn't interrupted. "They had promised each other, once, at the beginning, to love each other forever, to the grave and beyond—which was the sort of thing they used to say back then. Very emotional people, the Victorians. They wove jewelry out of their hair, you know, to be remembered after they died."

"But it says she died for love of him," Harrison insisted. "I saw her." There, he'd said it out loud. "I saw her crying for him."

Mr. Sonneman shook his head. "I've seen her, too. She cries for herself, Harrison. She said she'd love him forever. He held her to that. He waited two days after he died, and then he came for her. They heard her scream, but her door was locked. They had to break it down. They found her strangled, in a room no living person could have entered. She didn't die for love of him. She died for *promising* to love him.

"The dead can be very jealous, you know. Some of them. They get lonely in their graves and come looking for company. They whisper lies in your ears. They feed on your own doubts and weaknesses until there's nothing left of you at all."

"That's an awful thought!"

"Some of them." Mr. Sonneman shrugged. "There are ghosts and then there are ghosts. You know you're loved, don't you, Harrison? They couldn't fool you with those lies, could they?"

Harrison looked away in shame, thinking of his parents, of his friends—of a hundred ways they had shown their love for him over the years.

"Sunday was the hundredth anniversary of his death. Today is hers. They'll have less hold on you tomorrow. Even less now that you know. They won't be able to manipulate your emotions anymore."

Harrison shuddered, remembering the tears that had stung his eyes as though they'd occurred a long time ago, to someone he no longer was.

"I'll get off here," Mr. Sonneman said. "Go home." He patted Harrison's shoulder. "Rest."

Finally he got his mouth to work, but by then Mr. Sonneman had already walked halfway up the hill, where he couldn't follow with his bike, or at least not easily. "Wait!"

"Not all the dead are like that," Mr. Sonneman called back.

"But how do you know . . . ?" Too late. He was already gone.

Very strange, Harrison thought.

And thought it again the following week when he started to ask Mr. Reisinger about his old partner Charlie Sonneman and his peculiar view regarding jealous ghosts. Mr. Reisinger only shook his head and told him Charlie had died last fall.

*Not many kids have a friend who can tell stories
like Ichabod Hanson can. . . .*

GHOST STORIES

Lawrence Watt-Evans

"Oh, sure, Damon, the old Hanson place is really
haunted, but you go there anyway," Jeremy said
sarcastically. "You play with the ghosts, right?"

"There's just one ghost," Damon said. "His
name's Ichabod Hanson, and yeah, we play
checkers, or cards, and he tells me stories and
stuff."

"Right," Jeremy scoffed. "And my teacher is
Madonna in disguise. She gave up music to teach
sixth grade."

"You don't believe me?" Damon asked with
a peculiar smile.

"Of *course* not!" Jeremy replied.

"Come on, then. I'll show you."

Jeremy didn't like the look on Damon's face,
and he didn't like the look of the Hanson house,
but he couldn't refuse a challenge like that.

"Okay," he said. "When?"

"What's wrong with right now?" Damon asked.

Jeremy blinked in surprise and looked around at the bright sunshine. "Does the ghost come out during the day?"

Damon shrugged. "Sure."

Jeremy couldn't see any way out. "Okay," he said.

The old Hanson place had been built more than a hundred years ago—Jeremy had heard his mother say so—and it looked as if it hadn't been painted or repaired in all that time. It was all weathered gray wood, with just a few shards of glass left in the narrow windows.

The two boys parked their bikes in the tall grass by the porch, and Damon led the way up the sagging steps. The boards creaked under their weight. Jeremy tried to be as light as he could— the ancient planks felt as if they might break at any moment.

The front door stood open, and Damon stepped inside. "Hi, Mr. Hanson?" he called. Jeremy stood nervously on the porch peering in; Damon leaned back out and whispered, "Listen, let me do the talking. Don't you say *anything*. Okay?"

Jeremy, who was beginning to think this might be more serious than he liked, nodded nervously.

"Come on inside," Damon said.

Warily Jeremy stepped in—and the door closed behind him, all by itself.

He moaned.

He'd always thought most horror movies were stupid because nobody would be dumb enough to just walk right into those traps where the monsters could get them, the way the people in the movies always did, but here he'd gone and walked right into a haunted house, and now the ghost was going to get him. . . .

But Damon didn't look scared at all.

"Good day, young Damon," a strange voice said, and Jeremy jumped. " 'Tis a pleasure to see ye. Who might this other lad be?"

"Hi, Mr. Hanson," Damon said cheerily. "This is Jeremy." He nudged Jeremy. "Say hello," he whispered.

Jeremy said, "Uh . . . hi," to the empty air.

"A good day to ye, Jeremy," the voice said, and this time Jeremy could see him, an old man at the top of the stairs, with the sunlight from an upstairs window coming right through him—a rather small man, with a bushy beard and curly hair worn fairly long. He had on an old-fashioned black coat with big buttons, and a dark vest, and white pants. He was coming down the stairs toward them.

Jeremy backed up against the door.

"My name, as I suppose Master Damon's told ye, is Ichabod Hanson," the ghost said. "And

I'd offer to shake hands with ye, had I still a palm solid enough to grasp."

Jeremy glanced at Damon, but didn't say a word.

"Jeremy didn't believe I really knew a ghost," Damon said.

"I suppose 'tis a hard thing for some to believe," the ghost said, smiling through his transparent beard. "I'm none too sure I'd have credited it myself, when I was yet alive."

"Tell 'im how you wound up as a ghost," Damon suggested.

"Would you hear the tale, lad?"

Jeremy nodded, then stood staring at the ghost, listening.

"I was, y'see," the ghost said, "a sailor out of Boston, having gone to sea as a boy, a few years before the War Between the States, and a fine life I found it. I sailed the world around any number of times and saw every port from Halifax to Hong Kong, but a day came when it seemed to me that the time had come to settle down. So I built myself this house, and I found myself a wife, and I tried me best to live me a quiet life here on the land."

He sat down on the stairs and motioned at the boys; Damon promptly settled on the floor, and Jeremy cautiously followed his lead.

"I found, though," the ghost continued, "that the life of a landlubber was not for me. I'd a hankerin' to see foreign shores and strange sights

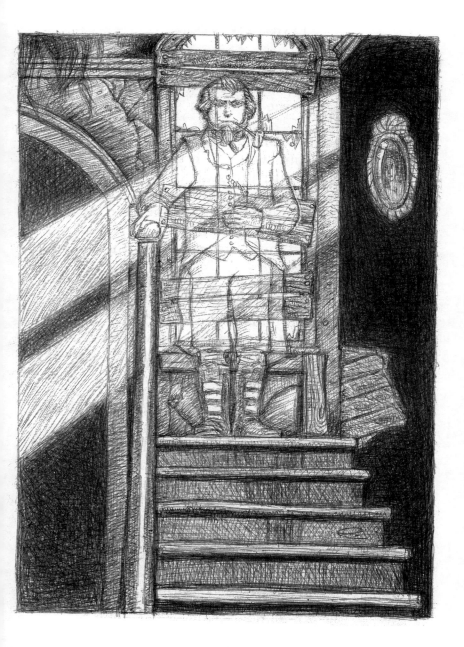

that was not to be denied." He sighed an intangible sigh. "So with a kiss and a farewell, I left me wife and me home and took ship for a run to Singapore."

He smiled with the memory. " 'Twas a fine voyage, lads, but when I come home, I was weighed down with the guilt of how I'd treated me missus, and I swore to her that I'd settle down for good and truly this time, and for another six months I did just that—but then an old shipmate offered me a first mate's berth on a tea packet. . . ."

And so it had gone, he explained, one voyage after another, and his wife had progressed from understanding to unhappy to angry, and, he said, he should have known better, for Mistress Sarah Hanson was from a family that was well known to have witchery in it.

"And at last," he said, "when I was perhaps a trifle too old to be traveling about as freely as all that, I told her one fine day that I'd a chance to captain a schooner on a run down to Rio de Janeiro, and she said she'd had quite enough of all that. She wanted her man at home, and where I'd got away from her before despite her asking and pleading and begging, she'd decided to resort to something a little stronger. And she put a spell on me, that I'd remain home here forevermore. And she didn't say until I died, neither—she said *forever*."

Jeremy glanced at Damon, and Damon smiled back.

"So I've been here ever since," Hanson said, "and all in all, I've not minded a bit—not even when I sickened and died. I'd thought that might be the end of it, but no, I was held here just the same. So I kept me widow company of an evening, telling her tales of my adventures in foreign ports—those tales that were fit for a lady, and some that weren't, and what's more, keepin' myself largely to the truth." He smiled at the memory. "And you know, lads," he said, "it seemed to me that I enjoyed the telling near as much as I'd enjoyed the doing—or perhaps a shade more. I'd no need to spend weeks between ports living in a crowded cabin smelling of bilgewater, getting from one place to another, as I had before."

All in all, he told the boys, he was grateful to his wife for the curse she'd put on him—save that it had been lonely when she died, as no one had cursed *her.*

He paused for a moment, letting the lonesome silence sink in, then said, "But other folk happened along in time, and I enjoyed their company, told them a tale or two—just as I have Damon here, and as I'd be glad to tell *you,* Jeremy, if you'd like."

Jeremy nodded. "Yes, please," he said.

So Ichabod Hanson told Damon and Jeremy about his first visit to the Caribbean, as a boy of thirteen on a freighter hauling sugar, and how they'd run afoul of a hurricane and limped home with but a single mast and the hull full of water, and Jeremy listened to that, and thought he would gladly have listened forever, had not Damon eventually interrupted.

"It's past dinnertime," he said, pointing to the setting sun. "We'd better get home."

"Oh," Jeremy said, startled; he'd had no idea they had been there so long. "Oh, wow." He had been sitting cross-legged on the floor. Now he looked up at the ghost and said, "Wow, thanks, Mr. Hanson. It was a pleasure meeting you."

"Come back any time, lad. 'Tis a pleasure to have so attentive an audience as yourselves."

"Yeah," Jeremy said, "I will. I mean, it's too bad about the curse, but it's neat to hear all this stuff, you know?"

"Ah, the spell's hardly a curse, in truth, for my existence here's no hardship on me."

"Isn't there any way you can get out of it? Did she really curse you *forever*?"

"Oh, well, she done as good as, lad. The way of it was, we were talking, and she said I was the travelingest man she'd ever seen, and she saw no way that she could let me go the least little bit, for I'd be off to the far side of the globe in a trice if she even let me out to go to the market. And I said that I was no more besotted with travel than many another, and she'd stretched the truth of it. And she said that she'd never seen a man who'd gone as far as I, and never would until a man walked on the moon, and until then, I'd be cursed to stay inside these walls. So y'see, lad, 'tis as good as forever—I'm bound here until a man walks on the moon, and the word of it reaches me, and how could that ever happen?"

Jeremy's mouth fell open. "But my dad says . . ." he began.

Damon poked him, hard, in the ribs. Jeremy turned and saw a finger pressed to Damon's lips, so he didn't finish the sentence.

"Come on," Damon said, "it's time to go." He took Jeremy by the sleeve, opened the front door, and dragged Jeremy out onto the porch.

A few minutes later, as they were hurrying back toward their homes, Jeremy said, "But men *have* walked on the moon, years ago! My dad told me all about it! Why haven't you told him?"

"Because, you jerk," Damon said, "I haven't heard all his stories yet!"

Jeremy thought that over. It wasn't as if Mr. Hanson was in any hurry to move on. And Jeremy had hardly heard *any* of his stories.

"Right," he said. "Can I come back tomorrow? I promise I won't tell him."

Damon smiled. "Sure," he said, "any time."

*She's dead, but she's not hearing
an angel choir. . . .*

MRS. AMBROSEWORTHY

Jane Yolen

Specter.
Spook.
Phantom.
Phantasm.
Wraith.
Shadow.
Fetch.
Shade.

Those are all names for a ghost. I know. I
checked in the thesaurus. But what I saw coming
home from school choir practice didn't look a
thing like any of those. You know—misty white
and rattling chains. Or skeleton thin like the
walking dead. Or gibbering. Or drooling.

What I saw was the ghost of Mrs. Ambroseworthy, our old choir director, the one who was
drowned in the boating accident.

She was wringing her hair and muttering. She was not a happy lady.

Not that she'd been especially happy alive. She'd always been upset by Allen's high E or Melanie's low B or the altos coming in a beat too soon or the tenors a beat too late. She got mad when we missed a practice or when practice got canceled on account of a big basketball game. (The tenors were the basketball team, plus one bass.)

But I had never seen her so angry as I did a full five months after her body had washed ashore after the Fourth of July picnic at the lake.

"Mrs. Ambrose—" was all I got out of my mouth before sense and fear combined to silence me. But it was enough. She looked up and shook her finger at me, just as she used to when I sang out on the final rest, the one in the *Hallelujah Chorus.* "Gordon Wilson!" she said, only not aloud. Her mouth said the name and my memory supplied the sound. Mrs. Ambroseworthy had a voice hard to forget, both sharp and musical at the same time, sort of like a hand saw played in a band.

I turned and ran. I am not proud of that. But I'd been afraid of Mrs. Ambroseworthy when she was alive. Dead didn't make her any better.

Now ever since Mrs. Ambroseworthy's unfortunate death—*unfortunate* being my mother's word for it, not mine—Nancy Chapperel has led the choir. She's not much of a musician, but the entire football team now sings. They are, not surprisingly, all basses except for the quarterback. He can afford to be a tenor. Actually at least nine of them aren't really basses, but Ms. Chapperel lets them stay there anyway. Two of them aren't anything at all—bass, tenor, alto, *or* soprano—but she lets them sing as well.

Ms. Chapperel has long red hair that springs up around her face like a helmet and a 150-watt smile. She doesn't seem to notice when someone hits a note from the bottom up instead of from the top down. And she even has us singing a Christmas rap that she wrote herself, something Mrs. Ambroseworthy would spin in her grave about. If she *was* in her grave, which I doubted. Actually, the rap is truly stupid:

Here comes Santa in a two-ton semi,
Pedal to the metal, wha-wha and whammy,
Whammy, whammy, wha-wha-whammy. . . .

The backfield really likes that one. They were so rough on the *Hallelujah Chorus*, we had to drop it from the program. Which is too bad, since it was kind of a tradition. You know—once is a tryout, twice is a repeat, and three times is a tradition? Still, it's the first time so many upperclassmen have been part of the school choir, so no one is complaining. Especially not a middle-schooler like me.

But a ghost haunting the path behind First Baptist wasn't right. It wasn't comforting, either. I wondered what had caused Mrs. Ambroseworthy to come back now, almost half a year after her drowning.

Of course I didn't bother to do any of this wondering until I was safely home with the door locked and Mom's best garlic powder ground into the floor around my bed. Mrs. Ambroseworthy might have been some kind of bloodsucker, you know, disguised. I saw that in a movie on late-night TV. A guy can't be too careful.

Two days later, two nights of choir practice later, and the day before our Christmas performance, I was waiting for someone else to mention seeing Mrs. Ambroseworthy's wet ghost. She hadn't done anything to me but waggle her finger, but it wasn't like she was hiding or anything. She was simply out there on the path, in that old floral print dress, the one that Dad said made her look like she'd been upholstered rather than dressed. I'm not making this up, you know. She was definitely there. The ground underneath her was soaking wet. Yet for all that there were forty-seven kids in the choir (up from thirty last year because of the football team), no one said a thing.

Maybe, like me, they were afraid of being called cowards. Maybe, like me, they were afraid they were going crazy.

So I decided to broach the subject—that's

what my mom calls it when you kind of sneak up on something backward without actually committing yourself—during the Kool-Aid break in the vestry. We practice at the First Baptist Church because we've been performing there as well. It has an organ, a piano, and enough seats, which our school does not.

"So," I said, loud enough for at least half the tenors and all of the girls to hear me, "anyone here believe in ghosts?"

Three of the girls, including Tammie Lee, giggled. Tammie Lee put her hand over her mouth to do it. Her fingernails were like little pearls. Jimmy Stearnes punched me in the arm.

"Sure," he said. "And UFOs, too. Woo-woo!"

"I don't," I hastened to add. "Believe in ghosts, I mean." So much for broaching. "But I just wondered if someone here did?"

Lindsey Windsor—who we called Lady because she always wore dresses—raised her hand. Just like she wanted to be excused to go to the bathroom or something. "I do," she said, her face all scrunched up with the thought.

Just what I needed. Help from Lady.

"I do," she repeated, only in a very small voice. Lady Windsor always speaks in this tiny little voice so you have to lean toward her to hear what she's saying. Except when she sings. Then she has this incredibly pure soprano that simply soars over all the rest. She used to get all the solos B.C.—Before Chapperel, that is. It's hard to be a soprano singing rap. And the one soprano solo this year, in "O Holy Night," was transposed for the quarterback as a reward for admitting he was a tenor. Jack Armstrong. I kid you not. (Well, actually, his name is Geoffrey. Geoff Armstrong. But everyone calls him Jack the All-American Boy. And he did make All State in two sports.) He's the same guy who said, "Pitch is for wimps." And he didn't mean baseball.

"I do," Lady Windsor said again in her tiny voice, the voice that has been one seat behind me ever since first grade, Windsor coming right after Wilson. "I saw one."

"Saw one what?" I asked.

"She saw a ghost, a ghouly ghost," sang Tammie Lee. Then she giggled again, pearl-fingered hand to mouth. She looked like an oyster. The other girls giggled along with her. Sometimes I hate girls. Or maybe, as Mom says, I'm just not ready for them.

"It was Mrs. Ambroseworthy," Lady said.

The entire section leaned toward her, then leaned back, roaring with laughter. Forty-six kids roared altogether. That's forty-five plus me. I roared, too. I am not proud of that. I am pretty sure I was the only one who shouldn't have been laughing

Lady Windsor's face scrunched up some more and got shiny with tears. Then she ran out of the vestry and up the stairs. We could hear her feet running up the aisles and then the great *screak* of the front door opening and the *slam* of it closing after.

"I guess we weren't very nice," I said, only not real loud.

"Mrs. Ambroseworthy . . ." Jack Armstrong said slowly. "Didn't she drown?" He may be All State, but he's not All Smart.

"Last summer," Tammie Lee said, fluttering at him. "It was an accident."

"Accident," the bass section suddenly boomed in. "Ax, ax, accident." Like it was a new song.

"Not an ax, you yo-yos," I muttered. "A boat." But I said it very softly.

Just then Ms. Chapperel came in from the minister's office where she'd been working on some additional lyrics to the rap and handed them out. "I can tell you are eager, kids," she said. "So let's go. And—oh—did I hear somebody leave?" She watted her smile at us. Cute. Definitely cute.

Jack Armstrong was first as always. "Just Lady Windsor," he said.

"Why? Was she feeling ill?"

"I don't have a *ghost* of an idea," Jack said. Everyone laughed. Even me. I am especially not proud of *that*.

For a two-letter man, Armstrong is occasionally fast on his feet. And clumsy on everyone else's.

★ ★ ★

We struggled through the new lyrics. After all, we had only one night to learn them.

> Bringing to the good kids stockings full of candy,
> Soda pop and lemon drop and everything dandy,
> Dandy, dandy, dan-dan-dandy.

I didn't say Ms. Chapperel was a good writer. It didn't stop the entire bass section from grinning every time she lifted her arms for the downbeat.

The boys in the back row were hip-hopping to the music, and the risers began to shake. Ms. Chapperel had to caution them a couple of times. But as we plowed through the rest of the new verses, I almost hoped the whole place would collapse. The *Hallelujah Chorus* was looking awfully good in retrospect. Memory does that. Especially when memory has to contend with *these* lyrics.

Eventually choir practice was over, and we had to go home. It's a small town, and most of us walked. Even the upperclassmen. It's hard to convince your dad to lend you the car for the evening when First Baptist is right down the block.

Only Lady and I actually live behind the church, which means cutting through a backyard, through the old cemetery, and then on through Evers Copse, a silly name for a small if ancient stand of trees. Some Evers or other has always owned it. Of course we kids called it Every Cops, because every cop in town hides at the far end of it to catch speeders.

I would have walked the long way home, avoiding the yard and the cemetery, but it was an extra forty minutes because of the super highway and the swinging bridge and all. In the end I'd have to go through the copse anyway. And that's where Mrs. Ambroseworthy's ghost waited. Why there? I didn't know. My only other option was to stay all night in the church. My parents, of course, would have had a fit and, I suspect, around midnight would have had the police to First Baptist. I could have lived with that. But before I knew it, Ms. Chapperel had shooed us all out and sent us scattering away home, giving off that 150-watt grin and calling out, "Sleep well, kids. Tomorrow will be great."

So, dragging my feet, I went through the yard and straight into the cemetery. It had never been a scary place for us kids. We picnic there all the time. I checked Mrs. Ambroseworthy's grave, and it was undisturbed, though someone had put plastic flowers in a metal holder in front of it. The bright pink flowers looked odd against the snow.

There was nothing for it. I had to go through the copse. I took a deep breath and started.

And then I heard it. The crying. Loud and soft and loud again.

"Who's . . . who's there?" I called out.

"Gordon?" There was a sob at the end of it. I could barely hear my name.

"Lady?"

"Lindsey." (Sniff.) "I hate being called Lady." (Fade out.) Something white and fluttery started toward me, but it was only Lady . . . er, Lindsey's scarf.

"I've been waiting and waiting till you got here. And I'm awfully cold. But I just couldn't go through the trees on my own."

"Because of . . ." I asked.

"Because of . . ." She nodded.

Somehow it was even scarier not mentioning Mrs. Ambroseworthy's name.

"Why is she here, Gordon?"

I began to say "How should I know?" when the ghost suddenly appeared about ten feet away, as wet as ever, and wringing her hair. After about ten silent wrings, she turned and looked at us. Her eyes weren't red and shiny. She didn't have fangs or long nails. She didn't need them. She was scary enough on her own.

I found that my tongue had stuck to the roof of my mouth, like it was Super-Glued there. I couldn't have spoken even if I had wanted to. But Lindsey surprised me. Grabbing my hand and squeezing it for courage, she said in her tiny, quiet voice, "What do you want, Mrs. Ambroseworthy?"

Of course the ghost had to float a whole lot closer to hear her, and I just about passed out, but Lindsey kept holding on to my hand so I couldn't go anywhere.

I added my voice to Lindsey's. "What *do* you want?" My tongue was floppy in my mouth.

The ghost stared at the two of us and pointed her left forefinger up in the air, then pushed it higher and higher, the way she used to when anyone was flat. Usually me.

"You want me to sing higher?" Suddenly I had a quiver in my voice.

The ghost shook her head and water splashed everywhere, but none of it landed on us.

"You want to go up?" I asked. This time my voice was almost strong. "Like to Heaven?"

"Only you can't?" Lindsey whispered. I squeezed her hand back.

The ghost nodded.

"Can we help?" we asked together.

Mrs. Amброseworthy's ghost smiled, the same smile I had seen only once before, near the end of Lindsey's solo in "O Holy Night" when she hit that high note and held it, clear and pure and beautiful and long, long past the rest of us straggling behind her in harmony.

The night of the concert was one of those crisp, cold nights in December that make you think of Christmas cards. My mom and dad and little sister and I walked together to First Baptist. Dad held Mom's hand. I went on a little ahead so no one could know we were together.

Mrs. Ambroseworthy

The vestry was crowded with kids, all of us wearing white shirts or blouses because that's what looks best under the choir robes. Except for Jack Armstrong, whose shirt was more cream-colored.

"Because I've got the solo!" he said brightly. But his own color wasn't all that good. On his face, I mean. He was probably thinking about pitch. Mrs. Ambroseworthy had always cautioned soloists not to think too much before a performance. Just practice.

We filed onto the risers, and Ms. Chapperel stood up in her tight black dress and walked toward us. The audience applauded and the basses nudged one another, grinning.

We already knew the order of things. First a series of seven favorite Christmas carols, then a medley of pop Christmas tunes, like "I Saw Mommy Kissing Santa Claus" and "Jingle-Bell Rock." (I didn't say they were modern, just pop.) Then a break for juice, three Chanukah songs as a nod to multiculturalists, the rap song, and last, "O Holy Night," with Jack's solo. Just to be sure we remembered the new words for the rap, Ms. Chapperel had made large cue cards that stood on an easel facing us.

The carols went all right. They were old standbys, and those of us who had been in choir before had sung them all with Mrs. Ambroseworthy. If we were a bit ragged, it was because Ms. Chapperel was as nervous as we were, and hesitated once or twice on an upbeat. But I expect the only ones who noticed were Lindsey and me.

And Mrs. Ambroseworthy.

She stood in the back of the hall, behind a pillar, so no one could see her. But I spotted the puddle as it widened and deepened and began to creep down the aisle.

The pop tunes weren't too bad, either, though the tenors missed their entrance on "Jingle-Bell Rock" and the sopranos overpowered everyone on "All I Want for Christmas Is My Two Front Teeth."

Lindsey and I scarcely sang a note, and both the tenor and soprano sections sorely missed our direction. We were waiting, you see.

After intermission—and the church janitor tsk-tsking over the puddle and putting out a bucket because he thought melting snow had come through the roof—we climbed back onto the risers. Mrs. Ambroseworthy had disappeared, so nobody had seen her. My mom had twice wiped my face with her handkerchief, thinking I was sweating because of the concert, and I had almost been overwhelmed by the scent.

Lindsey looked at me and nodded. I nodded back. Sam Dougal noticed and elbowed me.

"Sweet on Lady?" he asked.

I stepped on his instep. Hard. It made him squeak out loud, and that brought a sharp look from Ms. Chapperel at the tenor section. Jack Armstrong was so nervous, he thought it was a look meant for him and stepped forward for his solo.

"Not *now!*" hissed Ms. Chapperel.

Jack turned beet red and stepped back up on the riser. He was shaking.

Now! I thought. *Mrs. Ambroseworthy. Now!*

But she didn't appear. The piano accompaniment began, and we plowed through Chanukah and launched into the rap.

"Here comes Santa," chanted the sopranos, the basses adding: "In a two-ton semi."

And *then* Mrs. Ambroseworthy stepped into view, behind the last rows. No one in the audience could see her, of course, as they were all looking at the choir. But she was fully visible to all of us kids.

The tenors got as far as "Pedal to the . . ." and then all the old members suddenly *really* noticed her. How could they not? She was wringing the water out of her hair.

They sang: "Puddle, puddle, pud-pud-puddle . . ." Then they quietly panicked and stopped singing altogether. Ginger Martin and Todd Benton began to moan, and Mary Martin McGee crossed herself three times and said a number of quick prayers never heard before at First Baptist. That left the football team, some of whom didn't recognize Mrs. Ambroseworthy and probably thought she was somebody's wet old aunt who had come in late. They kept struggling along with the song on their own. Of course, without the *real* singers, they just sounded like a bunch of monotones doing karaoke—which, in a way, they were.

The audience began to mutter.

Ms. Chapperel worked hard to pull us together, I'll say that for her. But when Ginger pointed and Ms. Chapperel turned around to see what was making Ginger gibber, the ghost disappeared—except for the puddle. So the choir began to straggle back onto the notes that the piano accompanist had doggedly kept playing. We forgot to do the extra lyrics, though, and Ms. Chapperel's 150-watt grin was gone as if a circuit breaker had been thrown.

And we still had one song to go, the song Lindsey and Mrs. Ambroseworthy and I had planned on. The one that would carry our old choir director to her perfect rest.

Ms. Chapperel signaled to Jack. "Now!" she whispered, clearly having decided she'd had a moment's weakness. Her grin was back in place. "Now!"

But Jack could not move. After all, he had recognized Mrs. Ambroseworthy. Though he'd never been in the choir before, he'd known her well. It had been his dad's boat she'd fallen out of before she drowned. Nervous about the solo to begin with, he was now as white as . . . well, as a ghost. Or as ghosts *should* be if they aren't Mrs. Ambroseworthy.

"Jack!" Ms. Chapperel stage-whispered.

This time he stepped forward, like a robot, and I was right behind him, a shadow, a shade, a wraith.

The piano began its arpeggios, up and down and up again, and just then Mrs. Ambroseworthy reappeared, her arms high above her head.

I tapped Jack on the shoulder and whispered, "Boo!"

He passed out and I caught him smoothly. From the front it looked as if I was a hero, catching him like that.

Lindsey stepped forward and sailed right into Jack's solo without missing a beat. Only—and this was unusual for her—she was slightly flat. Must have been nerves, from the rap and the ghost and all.

Ms. Chapperel sure didn't notice. She was just glad to get us all singing again. But we were ragged and Lindsey was flat. Mrs. Ambroseworthy, alive or dead, would never stand for that. And she didn't, either. She moved silently, swiftly, wetly, to right behind Ms. Chapperel, waving her own arms to get us back on beat.

I thought the audience would faint on the spot.

Then Mrs. Ambroseworthy lifted that warning finger and pointed to the ceiling. "Higher!" her voice hissed in my head.

Lindsey's shoulders suddenly straightened, as if she, too, had heard Mrs. Ambroseworthy's voice, and suddenly her soprano soared right on

to the perfect pitch, hitting it from the top down. And stayed there.

"Higher!" Mrs. Ambroseworthy said again in my mind, stabbing her finger into the air. And as I watched, she floated, smiling, as sure as Lindsey's voice up and up and up and up, heading for the ceiling of First Baptist and beyond.

We got a new choir director the next year, one who knew music and reinstated the *Hallelujah Chorus,* which I sang without a single mistake. Ms. Chapperel ran off to marry the coach of the college football team. Lindsey filled out, her voice got stronger, she forgave me all my instances of cowardice, and we have been going steady ever since.

But that's another story altogether. All-all-altogether.

*When I was young, my friends and I used to torment
each other with questions such as, "A terrible
fire is coming, and you can either escape without
your family, or stay and die with them.
What do you do?"
It's a bizarre kind of question (but, then, kids
are kind of bizarre). However, it also touches
on something important: For many people the
greatest fear is not their own death,
but the death of someone they love.
Joe Lansdale's story speaks to that fear in a
way that is both tender and macabre.*

NOT FROM DETROIT

Joe R. Lansdale

Outside it was cold and wet and windy. The
storm rattled the shack, slid like razor blades
through the window, door and wall cracks, but
it wasn't enough to make any difference to the
couple. Sitting before the crumbling fireplace in
their creaking rocking chairs, shawls across their
knees, fingers entwined, they were warm.

A bucket behind them near the kitchen sink

collected water dripping from a hole in the roof. The drops had long since passed the noisy stage of sounding like steel bolts falling on tin, and were now gentle plops.

The old couple were husband and wife; had been for over fifty years. They were comfortable with one another and seldom spoke. Mostly they rocked and looked at the fire as it flickered shadows across the room.

Finally Margie spoke. "Alex," she said. "I hope I die before you."

Alex stopped rocking. "Did you say what I thought you did?"

"I said, I hope I die before you." She wouldn't look at him, just the fire. "It's selfish, I know, but I hope I do. I don't want to live on with you gone. It would be like cutting out my heart and making me walk around. Like one of them zombies."

"There are the children," he said. "If I died, they'd take you in."

"I'd just be in the way. I love them, but I don't want to do that. They got their own lives. I'd just as soon die before you. That would make things simple."

"Not simple for me," Alex said. "I don't want you to die before me. So how about that? We're both selfish, aren't we?"

She smiled thinly. "Well, it ain't a thing to talk about before bedtime, but it's been on my mind, and I had to get it out."

"Been thinking on it too, honey. Only natural we would. We ain't spring chickens anymore."

"You're healthy as a horse, Alex Brooks. Mechanic work you did all your life kept you strong. Me, I got the bursitis and the miseries and I'm tired all the time. Got the old age bad."

Alex started rocking again. They stared into the fire. "We're going to go together, hon," he said. "I feel it. That's the way it ought to be for folks like us."

"I wonder if I'll see him coming. Death, I mean."

"What?"

"My grandma used to tell me she seen him the night her daddy died."

"You've never told me this."

"Ain't a subject I like. But grandma said this man in a black buggy slowed down out front of their house, cracked his whip three times, and her daddy was gone in an instant. And she said she'd heard her grandfather tell how he had seen Death when he was a boy. Told her it was early morning and he was up, about to start his chores, and when he went outside he seen this man dressed in black walk by the house and stop out front. He was carrying a stick over his shoulder with a checkered bundle tied to it, and he looked at the house and snapped his fingers three times. A moment later they found my great-grandfather's brother, who had been sick with the smallpox, dead in bed."

"Stories, hon. Stories. Don't get yourself worked up over a bunch of old tall tales. Here, I'll heat us some milk."

Alex stood, laid the shawl in the chair, went over to put milk in a pan and heat it. As he did, he turned to watch Margie's back. She was still staring into the fire, only she wasn't rocking. She was just watching the blaze, and Alex knew, thinking about dying.

After the milk they went to bed, and soon Margie was asleep, snoring like a busted chainsaw. Alex found he could not rest. It was partly due to the storm, it had picked up in intensity. But it was mostly because of what Margie had said about dying. It made him feel lonesome.

Like her, he wasn't so much afraid of dying, as he was of being left alone. She had been his heartbeat for fifty years, and without her, he would only be going through motions of life, not living.

God, he prayed silently. *When we go, let us go together.*

He turned to look at Margie. Her face looked unlined and strangely young. He was glad she could turn off most anything with sleep. He, on the other hand, could not.

Maybe I'm just hungry.

He slid out of bed, pulled on his pants, shirt and houseshoes; those silly things with the rabbit face and ears his granddaughter had bought him. He padded silently to the kitchen. It was not only the kitchen, it served as den, living room and dining room. The house was only three rooms and a closet, and one of the rooms was a small bathroom. It was times like this that Alex thought he could have done better by Margie. Gotten her a bigger house, for one thing. It was the same house where they had raised their kids, the babies sleeping in a crib here in the kitchen.

He sighed. No matter how hard he had worked, he seemed to stay in the same place. A poor place.

He went to the refrigerator and took out a half-gallon of milk, drank directly from the carton.

He put the carton back and watched the water drip into the bucket. It made him mad to see it. He had let the little house turn into a shack since he retired, and there was no real excuse for it. Surely, he wasn't that tired. It was a wonder Margie didn't complain more.

Well, there was nothing to do about it to-night. But he vowed that when dry weather came, he wouldn't forget about it this time. He'd get up there and fix that damn leak.

Quietly, he rummaged a pan from under the cabinet. He'd have to empty the bucket now if he didn't want it to run over before morning. He ran a little water into the pan before substituting it for the bucket so the drops wouldn't sound so loud.

He opened the front door, went out on the

porch, carrying the bucket. He looked out at his mud-pie yard and his old, red wrecker, his white logo on the side of the door faded with time: ALEX BROOKS WRECKING AND MECHANIC SERVICE.

Tonight, looking at the old warhorse, he felt sadder than ever. He missed using it the way it was meant to be used. For work. Now it was nothing more than transportation. Before he re-tired, his tools and hands made a living. Now nothing. Picking up a Social Security check was all that was left.

Leaning over the edge of the porch, he poured the water into the bare and empty flowerbed. When he lifted his head and looked at his yard again, and beyond Highway 59, he saw a light. Headlights, actually, looking fuzzy in the rain, like filmed-over amber eyes. They were way out there on the highway, coming from the South, winding their way toward him, moving fast.

Alex thought that whoever was driving that crate was crazy. Cruising like that on bone-dry highways with plenty of sunshine would have been dangerous, but in this weather, they were asking for a crackup.

As the car neared, he could see it was long, black and strangely-shaped. He'd never seen any-thing like it, and he knew cars fairly well. This didn't look like something off the assembly line from Detroit. It had to be foreign.

Miraculously, the car slowed without so much as a quiver or a screech of brakes and tires.

In fact, Alex could not even hear its motor, just the faint whispering of rubber on wet cement.

The car came even of the house just as lightning flashed, and in that instant, Alex got a good look at the driver, or at least the shape of the driver outlined in the flash, and he saw that it was a man with a cigar in his mouth and a bowler hat on his head. And the head was turning toward the house.

The lightning flash died, and now there was only the dark shape of the car and the red tip of the cigar jutting at the house. Alex felt stalactites of ice dripping down from the roof of his skull, extended through his body and out the soles of his feet.

The driver hit down on his horn; three sharp blasts that pricked at Alex's mind.

Honk. (visions of blooming roses, withering, going black)

Honk. (funerals remembered, loved ones in boxes, going down)

Honk. (worms crawling through rotten flesh)

Then came a silence louder than the horn blasts. The car picked up speed again. Alex watched as its taillights winked away in the blackness. The chill became less chill. The stalactites in his brain and mind melted away.

But as he stood there, Margie's words of earlier that evening came at him in a rush: "Seen Death once . . . buggy slowed down out front . . .

cracked his whip *three times* . . . man looked at
the house, snapped his fingers *three times* . . .
found dead a moment later . . ."

Alex's throat felt as if a pine knot had lodged
there. The bucket slipped from his fingers, clat-
tered on the porch and rolled into the flowerbed.
He turned into the house and walked briskly
toward the bedroom.

*(Can't be, just a wives' tale. Just a crazy
coincidence.)*

Margie wasn't snoring.

Alex grabbed her shoulder, shook her.

Nothing.

He rolled her on her back and screamed her
name.

Nothing.

"Oh, baby. No."

He felt for her pulse.

None.

He put an ear to her chest, listening for a
heartbeat (the other half of his life bongos), and
there was none.

Quiet. Perfectly quiet.

"You can't . . ." Alex said. "You can't . . .
We're supposed to go together. . . . Got to be
that way."

And then it came to him. He had *seen* Death
drive by, had *seen* him heading on down the
highway.

He came to his feet, snatched his coat from

the back of the chair, raced toward the front door. "You won't have her," he said aloud. "You won't."

Grabbing the wrecker keys from the nail beside the door, he leaped to the porch and dashed out into the cold and the rain.

A moment later he was heading down the highway, driving fast and crazy in pursuit of the strange car.

The wrecker was old and not built for speed, but since he kept it well tuned and it had new tires, it ran well over the wet highway. Alex kept pushing the pedal gradually until it met the floor. Faster and faster and faster.

After an hour, he saw Death.

Not the man himself but the license plate. Personalized and clear in his headlights. It read: DEATH/EXEMPT.

The wrecker and the strange black car were the only ones on the road. Alex closed in on him, honked his horn. Death tootled back (not the same horn sound he had given in front of Alex's house), stuck his arm out the window and waved the wrecker around.

Alex went, and when he was alongside the car, he turned his head to look at Death. He could still not see him clearly, but he could make out the shape of his bowler, and when Death turned to look at him, he could see the glowing tip of the cigar, like a bloody bullet wound.

Alex whipped hard right into the car, and

Death swerved to the right, then back onto the road. Alex rammed again. The black car's tires hit roadside gravel and Alex swung closer, preventing it from returning to the highway. He rammed yet another time, and the car went into the grass alongside the road, skidded and went sailing down an embankment and into a tree.

Alex braked carefully, backed off the road and got out of the wrecker. He reached for a small pipe wrench and a big crescent wrench out from under the seat, slipped the pipe wrench into his coat pocket for insurance, then went charging down the embankment waving the crescent.

Death opened his door and stepped out. The rain had subsided and the moon was peeking through the clouds like a shy child through gossamer curtains. Its light hit Death's round, pink face and made it look like a waxed pomegranate. His cigar hung from his mouth by a tobacco strand.

Glancing up the embankment, he saw an old, but strong-looking black man brandishing a wrench and wearing bunny slippers, charging down at him.

Spitting out the ruined cigar, Death stepped forward, grabbed Alex's wrist and forearm, twisted. The old man went up and over, the wrench went flying from his hand. Alex came down hard on his back, the breath bursting out of him in spurts.

Death leaned over Alex. Up close, Alex could

see that the pink face was slightly pocked and that some of the pinkness was due to makeup. That was rich. Death was vain about his appearance. He was wearing a black tee-shirt, pants and sneakers, and of course his derby, which had neither been stirred by the wreck or by the ju-jitsu maneuver.

"What's with you, man?" Death asked.

Alex wheezed, tried to catch his breath. "You . . . can't . . . have . . . her."

"Who? What are you talking about?"

"Don't play . . . dumb with me." Alex raised up on one elbow, his wind returning. "You're Death and you took my Margie's soul."

Death straightened. "So you know who I am. All right. But what of it? I'm only doing my job."

"It ain't her time."

"My list says it is, and my list is never wrong."

Alex felt something hard pressing against his hip, realized what it was. The pipe wrench. Even the throw Death had put on him had not hurled it from his coat pocket. It had lodged there and the pocket had shifted beneath his hip, making his old bones hurt all the worse.

Alex made as to roll over, freed the pocket beneath him, shot his hand inside and produced the pipe wrench. He hurled it at Death, struck him just below the brim of the bowler and sent him stumbling back. This time the bowler fell off. Death's forehead was bleeding.

Before Death could collect himself, Alex was up and rushing. He used his head as a battering ram and struck Death in the stomach, knocking him to the ground. He put both knees on Death's arms, pinning them, clenched his throat with his strong, old hands.

"I ain't never hurt nobody before," Alex said. "Don't want to now. I didn't want to hit you with that wrench, but you give Margie back."

Death's eyes showed no expression at first, but slowly a light seemed to go on behind them. He easily pulled his arms out from under Alex's knees, reached up, took hold of the old man's wrist and pulled the hands away from his throat.

"You old rascal," Death said. "You outsmarted me."

Death flopped Alex over on his side, then stood up to once more lord over the man. Grinning, he turned, stooped to recover his bowler, but he never laid a hand on it.

Alex moved like a crab, scissored his legs and caught Death above and behind the knees, twisted, brought him down on his face.

Death raised up on his palms and crawled from behind Alex's legs like a snake, effortlessly. This time he grabbed the hat and put it on his head and stood up. He watched Alex carefully.

"I don't frighten you much, do I?" Death asked.

Alex noted that the wound on Death's forehead had vanished. There wasn't even a drop of blood. "No," Alex said. "You don't frighten me much. I just want my Margie back."

"All right," Death said.

Alex sat bolt upright.

"What?"

"I said, all right. For a time. Not many have outsmarted me, pinned me to the ground. I give you credit, and you've got courage. I like that. I'll give her back. For a time. Come here."

Death walked over to the car that was not from Detroit. Alex got to his feet and followed. Death took the keys out of the ignition, moved to the trunk, worked the key in the lock. It popped up with a hiss.

Inside were stacks and stacks of match boxes. Death moved his hand over them, like a careful man selecting a special vegetable at the supermarket. His fingers came to rest on a matchbox that looked to Alex no different than the others.

Death handed Alex the matchbox. "Her soul's in here, old man. You stand over her bed, open the box. Okay?"

"That's it?"

"That's it. Now get out of here before I change my mind. And remember, I'm giving her back to you. But just for a while."

Alex started away, holding the matchbox carefully. As he walked past Death's car, he saw the dents he had knocked in the side with his wrecker were popping out. He turned to look at Death, who was closing the trunk.

"Don't suppose you'll need a tow out of here?"
Death smiled thinly. "Not hardly."

Alex stood over their bed; the bed where they
had loved, slept, talked and dreamed. He stood
there with the matchbox in his hand, his eyes on
Margie's cold face. He ever so gently eased the
box open. A small flash of blue light, like Peter
Pan's friend Tinkerbelle, rushed out of it and hit
Margie's lips. She made a sharp inhaling sound
and her chest rose. Her eyes came open. She
turned and looked at Alex and smiled.

"My lands, Alex. What are you doing there, and
half-dressed? What you been up to . . . is that a
matchbox?"

Alex tried to speak, but he found he could
not. All he could do was grin.

"Have you gone nuts?" she asked.

"Maybe a little." He sat down on the bed
and took her hand. "I love you, Margie."

"And I love you. . . . You been drinking?"

"No."

Then came the overwhelming sound of
Death's horn. One harsh blast that shook the
house, and the headbeams shone brightly through
the window and the cracks and lit up the shack
like a cheap nightclub act.

"Who in the world?" Margie asked.

"Him. But he said . . . Stay here."

Alex got his shotgun out of the closet. He
went out on the porch. Death's car was pointed

toward the house, and the headbeams seemed to hold Alex, like a fly in butter.

Death was standing on the bottom porch step, waiting.

Alex pointed the shotgun at him. "You git. You gave her back. You gave your word."

"And I kept it. But I said for a while."

"That wasn't any time at all."

"It was all I could give. My present."

"Short time like that's worse than no time at all."

"Be good about it, Alex. Let her go. I got records and they have to be kept. I'm going to take her anyway, you understand that?"

"Not tonight, you ain't." Alex pulled back the hammers on the shotgun. "Not tomorrow night neither. Not anytime soon."

"That gun won't do you any good, Alex. You know that. You can't stop Death. I can stand here and snap my fingers three times, or click my tongue, or go back to the car and honk my horn, and she's as good as mine. But I'm trying to reason with you, Alex. You're a brave man. I did you a favor because you bested me. I didn't want to just take her back without telling you. That's why I came here to talk. But she's got to go. Now."

Alex lowered the shotgun. "Can't . . . can't you take me in her place? You can do that can't you?"

"I . . . I don't know. It's highly irregular."

"Yeah, you can do that. Take me. Leave Margie."

"Well, I suppose."

The screen door creaked open and Margie stood there in her housecoat. "You're forgetting, Alex, I don't want to be left alone."

"Go in the house, Margie," Alex said.

"I know who this is. I heard you talking, Mr. Death. I don't want you taking my Alex. I'm the one you came for. I ought to have the right to go."

There was a pause, no one speaking. Then Alex said, "Take both of us. You can do that, can't you? I know I'm on that list of yours, and pretty high up. Man my age couldn't have too many years left. You can take me a little before my time, can't you? Well, can't you?"

Margie and Alex sat in their rocking chairs, their shawls over their knees. There was no fire in the fireplace. Behind them the bucket collected water and outside the wind whistled. They held hands. Death stood in front of them. He was holding a King Edward cigar box.

"You're sure of this?" Death asked. "You don't both have to go."

Alex looked at Margie, then back at Death.

"We're sure," he said. "Do it."

Death nodded. He opened the cigar box and held it out on one palm. He used his free hand to snap his fingers.

Once. *(the wind picked up, howled)*

Twice. *(the rain beat like drumsticks on the roof)*

Three times. *(lightning ripped and thunder roared)*

"And in you go," Death said.

A little blue light came out of the couple's mouths and jetted into the cigar box with a thump, and Death closed the lid.

The bodies of Alex and Margie slumped and their heads fell together between the rocking chairs. Their fingers were still entwined.

Death put the box under his arm and went out to the car. The rain beat on his derby hat and the wind sawed at his bare arms and tee-shirt. He didn't seem to mind.

Opening the trunk, he started to put the box inside, then hesitated.

He closed the trunk.

"Damn," he said, "if I'm not getting to be a sentimental old fool."

He opened the box. Two blue lights rose out of it, elongated, touched ground. They took on the shape of Alex and Margie. They glowed against the night.

"Want to ride up front?" Death asked.

"That would be nice," Margie said.

"Yes, nice," Alex said.

Death opened the door and Alex and Margie slid inside. Death climbed in behind the wheel. He checked the clipboard dangling from the dash.

There was a woman in a Tyler hospital, dying of brain damage. That would be his next stop.

He put the clipboard down and started the car that was not from Detroit.

"Sounds well-tuned," Alex said.

"I try to keep it that way," Death said.

They drove out of there then, and as they went, Death broke into song. "Row, row, row your boat, gently down the stream," and Margie and Alex chimed in with, "Merrily, merrily, merrily, merrily, life is but a dream."

Off they went down the highway, the taillights fading, the song dying, the black metal of the car melting into the fabric of the night, and then there was only the whispery sound of good tires on wet cement and finally not even that. Just the blowing sound of the wind and the rain.

(With thanks to Richard Matheson and Richard Christian Matheson)

Will a simple dare put Jasper in his grave?

JASPER'S GHOST

Nancy Etchemendy

I, Zachary Sheaffer, don't know whether anybody will believe this or not. Sometimes I can hardly believe it myself. That's why I'm writing it down—so I can remember everything that happened to me and Jasper Browning on Tuesday, May twenty-fifth, at Coleman School. I don't ever want to forget it, or convince myself it didn't really happen. After all, it's not every day you meet a ghost, let alone put one out of its misery.

When I got to school Tuesday morning, Eleanor Dubois was teasing Jasper, as usual. Eleanor's big for a sixth grader, and she's involved in everything from Tae Kwon Do to youth soccer. Name a sport, and she's better at it than any boy in the class. She and Jasper were standing under the tree house, looking up.

"Jasper, you're so totally lame, you couldn't make it up there even if you had a diesel crane," said Eleanor.

"Wanna bet? You're the one who can't make it." Jasper's face was so flushed I could barely see his freckles.

Eleanor had hit a real sore spot and she knew it. She grinned in a satisfied way. "Oh, yeah, right. Like you're gonna climb thirty feet up this rope when you can't even ride a Ferris wheel without screaming and barfing."

Two things have to be said here. One is that our whole class went to the carnival together last autumn, which is why Eleanor knew about Jasper and Ferris wheels. The other is that Coleman's a lot different from most schools. It's what parents call "an alternative school." We have no desks, no grades, and no homework. That doesn't mean we don't learn stuff. We learn plenty. We just have more fun doing it than is exactly usual. The carnival, for example, got me started on a project about centrifugal force, and the physics of the Tilt-A-Whirl, even though I generally hate science, but that's another story.

Coleman's located in a nineteenth-century mansion that looks more like a huge white wedding cake than a school. It also has the most awesome tree house imaginable. The tree house sits three stories up in the branches of an old oak tree. It was built, modified, and is still being added to by Coleman School kids. The *only* way to reach it is by climbing a thick, knotted rope from the ground. It's unbelievably scary getting up there, and most kids don't make it anywhere near the top till they hit seventh or eighth grade.

"Get outa my way, Eleanor!" said Jasper. He threw down his baseball cap and rubbed dirt on his hands.

Eleanor made a big deal of backing up and covering her eyes. "Oh, no!" she said in a smart, sarcastic voice. "I don't think I can stand to watch. You're just *so* brave and daring!" She laughed in a very mean way.

By this time Jasper was so furious that his freckles had completely disappeared. In fact, I could hardly tell where his face ended and his hair (which is about as red as hair gets) began. He was also scared spitless. His hands shook as he grabbed the rope.

I was beginning to think I ought to do something. I hate getting involved in other people's disagreements. But I knew how Jasper must feel. Eleanor picks on everybody. It's bad enough that she's a girl. What makes it truly putrid is the fact that she can kick a ball, throw a punch, and climb a rope. When Eleanor picks on people, they always end up thinking their only alternative is to do whatever it takes to prove she's wrong, even if they know she's right.

"Jasper, come on," I said. "You don't have

time for this. We're supposed to be painting sets for the play." It was the only thing I could think of. It was true, but unfortunately, it was lame.

"I'm supposed to be working on sets, too," said Eleanor, smirking. "But it's not going to stop me from climbing to the tree house if I want to."

I was beginning to feel a little desperate. "Jasper, let's go!" I called. "Maybe Eleanor wants to climb to the stupid tree house, but you and I have better things to do."

Jasper turned and snarled at me. No kidding. For the tiniest instant, his teeth showed between his lips, just like a dog's. I'm not sure I've ever seen him so angry and upset before. "Butt out, Zack! I'm gonna make it to that tree house if . . . if it's the last thing I ever do."

So much for trying to give a friend an easy way out.

Jasper started up the rope while Eleanor and I watched. He wasn't good at it. In fact, he was pretty clumsy, partly because he was shaking so hard. But he just wouldn't give up. The rope started swinging in slow, dizzy circles. The higher he got, the more it swung. He was getting shakier by the minute.

Then a very weird thing happened. As Jasper pulled even with the science room window on the second floor, something green appeared in the air just above him. I don't mean green like a bush or a tree. I mean *ectoplasm* green. I could see through it, and it shimmered, like a glow-in-the-dark curtain. It was only there for an instant, but that was long enough to tell that it was shaped like a boy. It had on shorts and a baseball cap and high-tops.

Jasper said, "Uuhhh," and shut his eyes. He stopped climbing and hugged the rope as if he were in love with it.

I glanced over at Eleanor, who had just finished wiping something off her shoe, but was now staring up at Jasper, her mouth half open. "Look how high he is!" she said.

I frowned. "What? Didn't you see that?"

She looked at me as if I were a total idiot. "Duh. Of course I see it. Jasper's farther up the rope than I've ever gotten, and I'm not even afraid of heights. I can't believe this."

"No. I mean that thing. The thing in the air!"

"Thing in the air? Hellooooh." She rapped the top of my head with her knuckles. "Anybody home in there? The thing in the air is your friend Jasper Browning."

Just then Jasper said, "Zaaaack." It came out long and shivery. "I don't think I can go any farther."

I was pretty confused, and more than a little annoyed at Eleanor, but Jasper was more important. "It's okay, Jas. Just come down," I said, trying to sound reassuring.

"I can't come down. I'm stuck. Help!"

Eleanor and I looked at each other. This was great. She was not only treating me like a wacko, she had also gotten poor Jasper stuck up a rope twenty feet off the ground. I was really mad at her, and I imagine it showed on my face.

"Why are you looking at me like that?" she said. "It isn't my fault. Nobody forced him to do it." She held her hands out, palms up, the picture of innocence.

"Go get help, Eleanor," I said.

For once in her life Eleanor closed her mouth and did what I asked. She ran around the corner and up the front steps, headed straight for the office.

I ran over and grabbed the end of the rope. At least I could keep it from swinging.

"Don't worry, Jasper. We'll get you down," I called.

But all I heard were Jasper's shaky sobs. Things were looking pretty bad. Now he not only had to suffer the humiliation of being helped down the rope, everybody was going to see him crying besides. I suspected that Jasper had seen the green thing in the air, too, just as I had, only closer. Whatever it was, it had scared him half to death.

I won't go into a lot of detail about how Jasper got down from the rope. I'll just say it involved the school custodian, the wood-shop teacher, the fire escape, and a bunch of mountain climbing equipment. Of course, all this activity drew a crowd of breathless onlookers. Some of the kids were really nice about it. The younger ones were pretty impressed by how high Jasper had climbed, and a lot of the older ones were, too. But of course there were some creeps who did things like flapping their arms and clucking chicken-style.

By the time Jasper's feet touched the ground, he felt so bad about himself that he couldn't even look anybody in the face. People were slapping him on the back and telling him it could happen to anybody. One eighth grader even came up to him and admitted that he'd never been brave enough to get as far as Jasper had. But you know how it goes. All Jasper seemed to hear were the mean things.

Even at Coleman, kids get in trouble for doing the kinds of stuff Eleanor and Jasper and I were doing when we should have been with the rest of the class, working on the play. I don't know what would happen to kids who caused a ruckus like that at a regular public school, but at Coleman, it meant Jasper and Eleanor had to go out and sit by the pond with Steven, our teacher, and talk things over. Meanwhile, I had to stay in from recess while the teacher's assistant, Terra, kept an eye on me. All this time I was dying to talk to Jasper myself to compare notes about the green thing. I couldn't sit still. I was just too anxious. Finally Terra gave up and made me go outside and run around the building three times.

*   *   *

At lunch I found Jasper sitting in a hidey-hole under a bush, chewing half-heartedly on a tuna sandwich and building mud dams with his orange soda.

"Hi," I said.

"Hi," he said, concentrating hard on his mud project.

"You know, anybody who calls you a chicken is just a butthead. You got farther up that rope than Eleanor ever has. You're not a chicken."

Jasper snorted and said, without looking at me, "Well, you're the only one who thinks so."

"No, I'm not. Besides, nobody else knows what they're talking about," I said. "Nobody else saw the ghost."

Jasper looked up in a flash, his eyes round. "You saw it? I was beginning to think I was crazy!"

I nodded. "I saw it, all right."

"Tell me what it looked like. How much did you see?" said Jasper. He spoke in a loud, excited whisper.

"It was green," I said. "And it looked like a kid. I didn't know there could be kid ghosts."

Jasper glanced uncomfortably in the direction of the tree house. I could see he was getting ready to tell me something big. I wondered how the world could sound so normal—birds tweeting, kids shouting, sprinklers running—when my heart was beating so hard and fast.

"Swear you'll never tell another living soul?" said Jasper.

"Cross my heart and hope to die, stick a needle in my eye," I whispered.

Jasper looked at me long and hard. "It's me."

"Huh?" I said.

"It's me! At least, it's the ghost of me." He shivered. "Its neck is broken and it's covered with blood."

The whistle blew and lunch was over. Jasper and I didn't get another chance to talk alone all day. Even though we both chose the same afternoon activity, clay studio, it was too loud and we were too busy to have a serious conversation. The talk by the pond was supposed to have fixed everything up between Eleanor and Jasper, but it hadn't really. Eleanor just wouldn't let up. Every chance she got, she called Jasper a baby or a coward, or bugged him in some other way. She took his baseball cap and climbed up the rope a little way and told him to come and get it. I had to hold him back. He was almost as mad at me as he was at her. He was having a really brutal day. The weird thing is, I think Eleanor actually likes Jasper but just can't figure out how to show it. So she does these stupid things just to get his attention. Whatever her reasons, they're not good enough.

Jasper had to go to the orthodontist after school, so I walked home alone. I don't live very far from Coleman, just across the street and a couple of houses down. I knew Jasper would be home about four o'clock, and I planned to call him.

Meanwhile, I did the usual after-school things. Mom had baked cookies, and she wanted to hear how my day went while I ate some. I told her about Jasper getting stuck, though I didn't mention the ghost. Then I had to play a game of Parcheesi with my dumb little sister, and I had to feed my animals. (I have a dog, a mouse, and a parakeet.) After that, I helped Mom set the table for dinner. Dad came home, and I had to tell him all about my day, just like I had with Mom. My parents are really big on hearing about everybody's day. Dad and I played a quick game of catch, and when we finished, it was time to eat. I didn't get around to calling Jasper till after dinner.

When Jasper's mom answered, I asked if I could talk to him.

"But . . ." she said, "I thought he was at your house. He left half an hour ago."

"My house?" I tried to think fast. It only takes Jasper about five minutes to ride his bike to my house. He had pretty clearly told his mom a lie. What was going on?

"Oh, hang on a minute. Somebody's at the door," I said, even though nobody was. I flattened my palm against the receiver. After a convincing length of time had passed, I put the phone to my mouth again and said, "Penny?" That's Jasper's mom's name. "He just got here. I guess he stopped off at the creek to look at tadpoles on the way."

"Okay," said Penny, though she sounded a little unconvinced. "Well, remind him he has to be home by eight-fifteen."

"I will," I said and hung up, feeling fairly slimy for having piled a new lie on top of Jasper's.

If Jasper wasn't home, and he wasn't at my house, then where was he? A few ideas were beginning to form in my mind, none of them very pleasant. I ducked into my bedroom to get my basketball, which I would need to convince my parents that I had a harmless reason to leave the house.

My bedroom has a big window that faces the street. Because we live just across from Coleman, I get a really good view of the school. As I was picking up my basketball, I looked out at the playground. I couldn't see everything, because there were too many trees in the way. And by now it was seven-thirty. Dusk was starting to fall. But I saw enough. There was Jasper, rubbing his hands together, getting ready to climb the rope again.

I raced for the front door. "I'm going over to the school to shoot a few hoops with Jasper," I called on my way out. Technically, it was another lie, but I figured it covered up Jasper's original one just about perfectly. Now there was no way he could get in trouble for it, unless he suddenly became amazingly stupid.

"Don't stay out too late," said Mom.

The air had that warm purple feeling it always gets the last few nights before school's out for the summer. Flowers bloomed somewhere nearby, sweet-smelling as candy. And the first crickets were out, chirping louder and louder as the sunlight faded. Something was going to happen. I could feel it in the back of my neck, like ants crawling.

Please let me get there in time! I thought as I sprinted toward the school. I ran so fast the wind plastered my shirt down and blew my hat off. Still, it seemed I would never reach Jasper.

All this time I was thinking about what it might mean for a person to see the ghost of himself. Was Jasper meant to die tonight? Would I arrive only to discover that he had fallen off the rope and broken his neck? I ran even faster.

I burst through the screen of oak trees and bushes that had temporarily blocked my view. And there was Jasper, just starting up the rope. He was already shaking. I must have been a hundred feet away, and I could still see how he trembled.

"Jasper!" I cried. "Wait! Don't do it!"

Jasper jerked his head toward me. That was when the green ghost appeared again, floating just below him. Luckily, Jasper was only a few feet up the rope. He was so startled that he let go and fell to the ground. By the time I arrived, he had picked himself up and was scuttling away like a scared crab, his eyes never leaving the ghost.

I ran up behind him, and he bumped into me. The basketball flew out of my hands and bounced across the playground. We both lost our balance and fell in a tangle, just a few feet away from the glowing green boy.

Jasper whimpered, "Wake me up! Oh, please wake me up!" I sure understood why he thought he was having a nightmare. The ghost was the most horrible thing I've ever seen. Its head was tilted at an impossible angle, and bones stuck out through the skin of its neck. Reddish-green blood poured from the wounds and dripped down its shirt. The worse thing of all was that it looked exactly like Jasper. It even had on the same shorts, cap, and high-tops he did.

I didn't think things could get any weirder, but just then they did. The ghost said, in a soft, echoey version of Jasper's voice, "Help me."

Jasper started to squirm away, raising a gritty cloud of dust around us.

I stared at the ghost's face. Those eyes were so terrible and sad that I had to think about what might be behind them. This glowing green kid had to be more than just a scary, evil creature. He was hurt so badly that he seemed beyond crying. Yet here he was, trying to tell us something.

I thought of something awful, and I couldn't

move until I had the answer. I coughed and swallowed dust. "How did you get this way?" I croaked.

"I got to the top. But I was shaking so much I couldn't get into the tree house. I slipped. It's so cold. I'm scared. Help me," said the ghost, and he began to shiver.

He switched his desolate, green gaze to Jasper. Jasper looked as if someone had just stuck him with a needle. His mouth opened and closed, but no sound came out.

"Why did we do it?" said the ghost. His eyes had begun to glow white hot. "Why?" he repeated, and this time his voice was loud and angry.

A couple of big tears crept out of Jasper's eyes and left shiny trails on his cheeks in the last rays of dusk. He crumpled his hair with both hands. I don't think he even noticed he was doing it. "I don't know," he said. "I feel like a wimp. Eleanor says I'm a chicken, and everybody else thinks it. I thought if I could make it up there . . . that would prove it wasn't true."

Jasper's tears were really coming. They ran down his neck and spattered the front of his shirt, just the way blood spattered the front of the ghost's. I wanted to do something, I don't know, maybe shake him and tell him I knew he was no chicken. But I had already done that while we ate our lunch. He hadn't believed me then, and I didn't think he would believe me now.

"You know we're not chicken. Why did you

believe it?" said the ghost. Now his tears started, too, like liquid emeralds on his cheeks.

"I don't know," moaned Jasper. "Leave me alone!"

"You took the easy way out," said the ghost. That really caught Jasper's attention. "What do you mean?" he shouted. "Easy! It's the hardest thing I've ever done in my life! I practically killed myself. . . ." His voice trailed off.

The ghost bent low over Jasper, who was still sitting on the ground. My hair stood up as he got closer. The air felt like it was full of electricity.

"The hardest thing to do is wait till you know you're ready, no matter what anybody else says. Help me, Jasper. Don't kill us," said the ghost, still shivering.

Jasper looked completely overwhelmed.

I saw my chance. "He's right, Jas. I've never made it to the tree house either, but *I* don't feel like a coward. Chicken is just a state of mind, and Eleanor Dubois is the biggest butthead in this town. You'll always be my friend!"

I didn't even know whether I was making sense or not. I just said the first things that came into my mind. But I guess they were the right ones, because Jasper scrubbed his knuckles across his eyes to get the tears away and socked me gently on the arm.

"Okay," he said. Then he looked up at the ghost. "Okay, go away now. *Please!* You win. I'm not gonna climb the stupid rope." He sniffed and wiped his nose on his shirt.

He and the ghost, and probably me, too, grinned huge grins at the same time. With a little popping sound, as if someone had pulled a cork out of a bottle, the ghost disappeared.

Jasper and I got up and hunted around till we found my basketball. Then we walked home, talking all the way.

And that's where the story ends. Except I ought to say that the next day at school, when Eleanor started bugging Jasper about the tree house again, he just made a face and said, "Eleanor, I don't feel like climbing it. If it's such a big deal, climb the rope yourself."

Later in the afternoon Eleanor passed Jasper a note saying she had decided he wasn't really a chicken, and asking if he'd like to work on a journal project with her.

The ghost has not been seen since.

*As a former gravedigger, I found this story
particularly amusing. . . .*

THE SECRET OF CITY CEMETERY

Patrick Bone

Only kids believed City Cemetery was haunted. But
that changed the Halloween night fourteen-year-
old Willard Armbruster disappeared. His body
was never found.

Willard was a bully. He had no friends. There
wasn't a kid in school who would play with him.
But Willard didn't mind. He liked being a bully.
The older he grew, the better he became at it.

Once, he told Wylma Jean Kist that her
mother had been run over by a subway train. It
took Wylma Jean weeks to get over Willard's
joke. That didn't bother Willard. It just made him
want to invent meaner pranks to play on people.

That's why he was beside himself with glee
when he saw city workmen digging graves at the
edge of the public cemetery. They were paupers'
graves, intended for persons whose families

couldn't afford the fancy plots near the center of the cemetery. Several graves were dug before winter frost would make digging difficult. Willard knew they would be filled in as needed.

He was clever enough to see that the part of the cemetery where the graves had been dug was located next to the playground of Mark Twain Middle School. The sidewalk leading into the school playground and up to the front entrance ran beside the freshly dug graves. There was no way a kid could go in or out of the playground or school building without passing by the graves.

When weather permitted, smaller neighborhood children always played in the schoolyard till dark. Willard didn't believe in ghosts. But he knew most of the kids did. He counted on that.

One evening, just before dark, he snuck into the graveyard next to where some kids were playing catch on the school playground. Fall had set in, and the days were growing darker. Willard hid near the freshly dug graves. At sunset the kids started to leave. Dark clouds hovered overhead. Wind whistled eerily through the trees.

"Perfect!" he snickered as he lowered himself into one of the graves, using a small stepladder he had stolen for the occasion. As the kids walked near the graves, he moaned in a pathetic, pleading voice, "Help me! I'm still alive! Nooo, nooo. I'm alive! Please help me!"

The kids screamed all the way home, where

they told their parents that someone was buried "alive" in one of the graves.

At first none of the parents took them seriously.

"Ghost stories," they all agreed. "Overactive imagination," some said. But when Willard played the trick again, a few parents called the police. Willard was long gone when they went out to check. After a while no one paid any attention to the kids. Police stopped checking, and the students at Mark Twain got used to the trick. They decided no one was actually buried alive. It was the ghost's way of haunting them from the graveyard.

Willard had fooled everyone. At least, that's what he thought.

One evening just before the cemetery closed, Henry Grasmick, the graveyard caretaker, saw Willard sneaking into the cemetery again. Henry always ignored the occasional kid who ran in and out of the graveyard to tempt the ghost and brag about it. But what Willard had been doing was not only tempting, it was cruel. So Henry crept up behind Willard and whispered, "I know what you're up to, boy."

Willard jumped as if a spider had crawled up his pants. When he saw it was Henry, he didn't act as if he was afraid. "Get away from me, you ugly old man," he said, and spit right at Henry's shoes.

Henry wasn't intimidated. "You don't know

what you're getting into, boy. It ain't no good to mess with the ghost."

Willard laughed. "What ghost? I never saw any ghost. Even if one does exist, he can't do anything to me. Ghosts are spirits, old man. They can't touch me. But I can touch you"—he raised his fist—"which is exactly what I'll do if you snitch on me!"

Henry ignored the threat. "Don't mess with the ghost," he repeated. "He does exist. He has his ways. Since I was a boy I worked here, and he left me alone. But I never messed with him." Henry turned as if he were about to leave. "You don't have to worry about me telling on you, young man. You only have to worry about what the ghost is going to do to you if you keep coming here."

Henry's warning had some effect, because Willard did stop his tricks at the cemetery for a time. But he stayed busy elsewhere.

He almost got away with some vandalism at school, but became too sure of himself and was caught and placed on a week's detention. He got bored. On his last day of detention he flushed a cherry bomb down a third-floor toilet, shattering the commodes on every floor below. School psychologists had to be called in to counsel the kids who happened to be sitting on the pots when they exploded.

Willard was proud of his pranks, but he could never forget the excitement of playing dead in an open grave. He was soon to get the thrill of his life.

Halloween night the middle school had a haunted house. To Willard, that meant one thing. Most of the kids would be there. He was delighted. Everyone who came would have to walk down the path past the open graves. *No more small-time tricks,* he thought to himself. *This time I scare all the kids.*

He arrived early at the cemetery and lowered himself into one of the graves, staying low so no one would see him. He even put his stepladder on the ground under him to make sure it was out of sight.

The sun set. Willard watched the darkness close over his grave like a shroud. He shivered and cursed the cold. It had rained earlier. He smelled the moldy mud squishing under his feet. Suddenly he heard footsteps. He was about to scream out, "Help me! I'm still alive!" But he realized the footsteps were coming from *inside* the cemetery, and not *outside* on the children's path.

He froze, not from the night chill.

Is it the police, he thought, *or someone else who has discovered the tricks I've been playing?*

Now *he* was afraid, and the fear of being discovered was more than he could take. So he huddled there, as far down in the grave as he could, hoping whoever it was would go away without finding him. But the footsteps didn't go away. They got louder, and closer.

Maybe it isn't the police, he thought. *Maybe it isn't . . . even human!* Or *maybe . . .* He didn't want to consider that maybe he had gone too far in mocking the dead.

In his mind Willard could hear the old caretaker's warning: *"Don't mess with the ghost, boy. The ghost has his ways."*

The footsteps were closer now. They were heavy steps. Soon Willard realized there were several sets of footsteps, coming directly to his grave. He was too terrified to scream. All he could do was stare up at the mouth of the grave and wait. Suddenly, just above the grave, he heard groans, heavy breathing, shuffling, and grunting sounds.

That's when he saw it. Something long and large and black hovered over him, then inched toward him into the grave.

It took Willard a split second to realize *It's a coffin!* and less than that to scream, "No! Please! I'm down here!"

All four gravediggers reacted the same way. They dropped the ropes holding the coffin and ran for help. The coffin fell like dead weight, directly on Willard—*thump*—knocking him cold.

Minutes later the cemetery superintendent showed up with the gravediggers to inspect the grave.

"There's nothing down there but a coffin,"

he said. "Boys, I ain't got time for ghost stories. The only spirits in this graveyard are the ones you've been drinking. Now, why don't you just bury that body."

When Willard came to, he discovered the "trick" was on him.

Every Halloween since, school children have claimed they could hear the muffled screams of the Ghost of City Cemetery, begging to be released.

"Help me! Please, help me, I'm alive! Noooo, noooo. I'm alive! Pleeease! Don't leave me here!"

When a ghost comes to visit, the past and the present mix in strange ways.

THE GHOST IN THE SUMMER KITCHEN

Mary Frances Zambreno

When the little girl first visited the summer kitchen, I didn't realize that she was a ghost. It was Sunday, and I was baking pasties for my father to take with him to work during the week. Making pasties is hot work, so I'm always glad when I can use the summer kitchen. The little log building out in back has an iron woodstove and screened-in windows on all four sides. It would get uncomfortably hot with cooking as the day wore on, but not unbearably so, and at least the house would stay cool.

I was rolling out the stiff dough for the crust, as my mother had taught me, when there was a shadow from the doorway.

"Hello," said a strange girl, outlined against the morning sun. "What are you doing?"

I froze, staring at her with more than a little rudeness. She was a few years younger than I was, about my little sister Sara's age, and she was wearing a thin white dress that looked like a nightgown. Her fair hair hung loose down her back, and her feet were bare.

"Who are you?" I asked sharply. I'm not used to being surprised by strangers when I'm cooking. And after all, our nearest neighbor lives half a mile down the paved road from us. "Where did you come from?"

The girl drew back from the door, her eyes widening slightly.

"I didn't mean to bother you," she said. She sounded frightened, and I was sorry for it; I hadn't meant to scare the child. "I'm Annie Pennick. I'm visiting my grandmother because she's sick. I just wanted to see what this funny little building was, and then—I'm sorry. I'd better go."

Moving more quickly than I could speak, she slipped away and down the hill. I would have called after her then, and apologized for having spoken so sharply, but there wasn't time. In a moment I was glad that I'd kept my mouth shut.

It was as I was watching her out of sight down the hill that it happened. First the white nightgown started to shimmer, as if a fog had passed over the sun. But the day was bright and warm, with achingly blue sky behind the deep green of the pines, and never a cloud in sight.

Then her long golden hair started to shiver with light, and fade from gold to silver to white to—

Nothing. She was gone. I blinked and rubbed my eyes, but there was no fair-haired little girl running down the hill. She had vanished as if she had never been.

Well, I may be only fourteen years old and not as sharp as I think I am (or so Aunt Grace is always telling me), but I know a ghost when I see one. Mother had often spoken of the summer kitchen as haunted. Before she died, she'd said that she saw spirits over this way whenever she was wakeful at night, and that that was how she'd know when her time was coming. I hadn't exactly believed her then, she'd been so weak and even feverish much of the time, but now ... I felt a shiver trickle down my spine.

Perhaps I should have gone for help right then. But what could I have said? There was no proof that anyone had been in the summer kitchen with me, not even a bare footprint in the dusty earth outside the door. And anyway, who would I have told? Aunt Grace? She would never believe me. Aunt Grace wouldn't believe me if I said that the sky was blue and winter was cold. Father was at work, and the children were no help—Elizabeth and Sara had taken little Ben to the Makis' farm, to see the animals. They'd play with the Maki girls and help with chores, too, and probably finish by bringing home fresh eggs. That was more important than my fears.

And the ghost hadn't *seemed* threatening. She was no taller than my sister Sara, and with Sara's big blue eyes and golden hair, too. Surely she couldn't mean any harm? So long as she didn't frighten the children . . . but then, would they be afraid of another child? I doubted it. More likely they'd see her as another playmate and would frighten *her* away, as I had done. And Father had enough to worry about. The mines had been on strike for part of the spring and were only just back to full production. We'd small enough savings to get by, without him thinking that it wasn't safe for me to be alone most of the days, and spending good wages on a housekeeper. He fretted enough about that as it was.

I really don't mind being alone during the day. It's mostly only when the children are at school, and not so bad during the summer. At Mother's funeral Aunt Grace asked me if I wouldn't rather come to live with her in town— she said that Father could easily hire a woman to tend the little ones—but I told her firmly to mind her own business. Why should I do Aunt Grace's washing and ironing and cooking and cleaning, instead of doing it all for my own family? That was what she had in mind, of course; she knew how well Mother had taught me, much better than she'd taught her own lazy daughters.

Besides, it isn't as though Ironvil were a big city. We're just a little mining town on the shores of Lake Superior—there isn't much to do except dig for iron and chop down pine trees for timber. Living in town is much like living just outside of it, only outside we have room for a proper garden. Even Aunt Grace had to admit that my garden was something special. This year I would have rutabagas and beans and lettuce and tomatoes and carrots and sweet basil and red and yellow cabbages, and of course potatoes and onions enough to share with all the neighbors. I had meant to try squash, but hadn't got the seeds into the ground in time. That was my only failure, though. Even the old raspberry bushes looked as if they would be heavy with fruit by mid-July.

So in the end I held my peace about the ghost. In a way, I was sorry that she'd left so quickly. Mrs. Jenks, the minister's wife, says that ghosts walk because they are unquiet spirits and need to finish something that they should have done in life. Reverend Jenks says it's foolishness and not to listen—he even scolded her at the church picnic for talking like that—but I wasn't so sure that I agreed with him. I would regret frightening the poor little girl ghost away from finishing some task that she needed to accomplish before she could rest. It must be a terrible thing, to be an unquiet spirit, I thought, and one so young at that. Privately, I wondered how she had died, and if she was unhappy. I would have liked to help her, if I could. I wondered if she'd come again, though I'd of course no way of knowing. If I'd had a clue as to why she'd come in the first place, I might have guessed—but I didn't, and that was that.

Until she *did* come back, about two days later. I was boiling the jars to get ready for raspberry preserving season—it really looked like being a bumper crop of berries, though the bushes were older than I was—when I saw her shadow in the doorway again. She was wearing the nightgown again, and the sun shining behind her made her look as if she were glowing in the morning light. Perhaps she was.

I managed not to look up from my work, though it was an effort to keep my hands moving.

"Hello," I said and was proud that my voice was steady. I could feel the pulse beating in my throat, and I had to work to breathe evenly, but I didn't want to scare her off this time. Not until I'd found out a few things. "I was wondering if you'd come back. Would you like to sit down and stay a while?"

"I don't—know if I can," she said, sounding puzzled. She moved in from the door, as lightly as a leaf on a spring breeze. "Am I dreaming? I feel as if I'm dreaming, sort of."

"I'm sure *I* don't know," I said—sensibly, I thought. Do ghosts dream? I'd have to ask Mrs. Jenks, the next time I saw her. I glanced up at the ghost. "Why don't you sit down and see?"

"I don't—want to bother you," she said, looking me full in the face for the first time.

"You won't bother me," I started to say, and then our eyes met, and the words went cold in my throat. An electric spark flashed from the ghost to me, burning me as it passed. A thin, invisible cord hung in the air, connecting us, making me feel as if she was a part of me as much as my sisters and brother were. I couldn't help it. My hands trembled, and the jar I was holding slipped between them to shatter on the floor. The sound broke the spell, if spell it was, and I jumped.

"Oh!" the girl said, and she was gone. Just like that—no fading into mist this time, just disappeared between one breath and another.

I stood for a long while, staring at the space where she had been, before I realized that I'd been holding my breath and let it out slowly. The question was, who was she? Annie Pennick, she'd said. Pennick was a Cornish name, not uncommon in these parts. "Seek ye by Tre, by Pol and Pen, for thus shall ye know the Cornishmen," says the old rhyme. And Anne, or Anna, is not an uncommon name. My mother's name was Anna, in fact, and it's my own middle name, though I've always been called Rose. Father used to call me his Wild Rose of the North Country, because I loved to go hunting and fishing with him so much—though I'd no time for such amusements any more. . . .

But the ghost. Who could she be? Someone who had lived in this house before us? That was possible. It's an old house, though sturdy, and we just rented the land that it stood on, from the mines. Possibly it had even been moved from one of the rows of company houses, over on the other side of town; the structure was similar, and people often moved houses. Why, there was a wealthy woman in Marquette who'd had her great mansion taken apart and shipped, stone by stone, all the way to the east coast—just because she was angry with her neighbors. People who survive on the shores of Lake Superior tend not to let a little thing like picking up a house and moving it down the road stop them from living where they want to live. Any number of families could have called this house "home" before us.

And probably had, since miners' families tended to move even more often than miners' houses. If this little Annie had been a miner's daughter, her father might have died in a cave-in. I didn't recall the name from any of the lists of the lost, but it might have been when I was too young to remember. Or no, wait, she'd said she was visiting because her grandmother was dying. Did I know of any ailing old ladies in town? Perhaps. There were always a few widows about, with or without grandchildren. It's a difficult life for a woman, being married to a miner, but the ones who survive the early years and childbirth usually live to a great age. We have to be tough, we northern mining folk. If Mother hadn't had Benjamin, she might—no. That was no way to think. Mother lived long enough to see to it that I knew how to take care of the family, to teach me to cook from Grandmother's recipe book, and to sew and clean by her own exacting standards. I would teach Sara and Elizabeth, and my own daughter someday, who would teach hers in turn. . . . The family was what mattered.

Or perhaps the "grandmother" whom the ghost referred to was long dead, and she was simply confused. It was difficult to guess without more information. This time, however, I didn't wonder whether or not she would come back. I knew that she would. And sooner or later one of the children would see her and perhaps be frightened, and Father would be upset.

That wasn't good. I had to find out why little Annie Pennick couldn't rest, and then see to it that she could. If I could. I still hadn't figured out what she wanted from me, but I was beginning to have an idea. Why else would she come to the summer kitchen, and only when I was cooking there? This would bear thinking on—unless next time she came someplace else.

She didn't. It was on a Saturday, baking day, when Father had taken the children out to the woods with him to keep them out of my way. Baking day is always a tricky business, even in the summer kitchen, and I was late. I often overslept on Saturdays, because Father was around to see to the early morning chores.

Mother wouldn't have approved, but she would have understood how tired I was. Anyway, that was why I was still kneading the first batch of bread, before setting it out to rise, when I suddenly realized that I wasn't alone.

I looked up. The ghost was standing in the doorway, as usual, but this time she was a few steps inside. She smiled uncertainly.

I swallowed. "Come in," I said, as warmly welcoming as I could be. I'd had several days to think of what to say, and I knew that this was important. Knew *what* was important, too—first things first. "Please. Don't leave—if you mean no harm, I mean no harm."

She hesitated. "I don't mean any harm to anyone, I don't think . . . but who are you?"

"Rose Palmer," I told her gravely. She started a little at that, and I wondered if she'd known the name of the person she was visiting. Perhaps not, if it was only that she'd lived in our house once upon a time. "I live here."

She looked around the summer kitchen. "In here?"

"No, of course not." I chuckled. It was going just as I'd planned. "This is just the summer kitchen. I cook out here, when the weather gets too hot. The big house is behind us, up the hill."

"I see." She seated herself on the bench near the wall, carefully, as if sudden movements—even her own—might frighten her. I hadn't imagined a shy ghost before, but why not? Careful, now, I told myself. Don't rush things. Let her make the first move. "What are you doing?" she asked.

I waved at the bread dough. "I've been kneading bread. Then I'll cover it and set it to rise, and pretty soon I'll be able to punch it and shape it."

"You're baking bread?" Her brow wrinkled. "Do you like to bake?"

I shrugged. "It's all right. Better than some chores—canning, for instance. I hate canning."

"Then why do you do it?" she asked, sounding confused. "I mean, if you don't like it . . ."

"Well, *someone* has to do it," I said. What a strange question, even for a ghost. "Or else we wouldn't have food in the pantry next winter."

She was quiet for a few minutes, watching me work. That suited me; I did need to pay attention to my bread, and I also needed time to think what next to say. I had a chance now, but I wasn't sure. . . .

When the dough was covered and set to rise, I was ready.

"How is your grandmother?" I asked casually. "You said she was ill."

For a moment I didn't think she was going to answer. Then she said: "The doctor says she's as well as can be expected. She doesn't really know anyone anymore—just sleeps all the time. I never even got to say good-bye."

"That's sad," I said, wiping my hands on my apron. "But surely you said good-bye the last time you saw her."

Annie shook her head. "I was really little. She let me bake cookies with her, and said the next time I came to visit we'd do some more, but then we moved to Chicago and I never saw her again. She used to send presents for my birthday and Christmas, and Mother kept saying we'd visit, but we never did."

"Why not? Chicago isn't far." This was it, I realized—my best chance, the one I'd been hoping for. If she'd never gotten a chance to say good-bye to her grandmother, then that was why she was unquiet. But how could she say good-bye now? She was trapped. I thought I saw a way out, but it would be tricky. It all depended on whether I was right about her coming to the kitchen. "You could have come up on the train."

"I think it was the divorce," Annie said, looking away. "Mother visited sometimes, but after she and Dad got divorced, I had to stay with him in California over the summer, and—I couldn't come during the school year."

I thought about that for a while. Divorce was a terrible thing, I'd heard—Reverend Jenks could get quite upset on the subject—and California was a terrible long distance, but it seemed hard to deny a child visits with her grandmother because of it. Still, I had my opening.

"You said you used to bake cookies with your grandmother," I said. "Well, I'm baking today. Would you like to help me? Sara sometimes does—

she's almost old enough to be a real help, and you look about her age."

She looked at me strangely. "Is Sara your sister?"

"Yes, my eldest little sister," I told her. "She's nine, five years younger than I am. Elizabeth is a year younger than she is, and Ben—my brother—is three years younger than that. There were two other babies in between Ben and Elizabeth, but they died. Sometimes it happens that way."

Annie took a deep breath. "I'm eleven now. So I guess I'm old enough to learn to bake for real."

Well, of course she was. Eleven! I couldn't believe that her mother hadn't started teaching her already. I found her a spare apron from the hook on the wall—one of Mother's old ones, but we pinned it up so it didn't drag on the floor. She seemed much more solid now, made of flesh and blood instead of mist and sunlight. Perhaps it was that she was doing something that would help her. I hoped so. Or perhaps it was just that we were baking bread. There is something about bread that makes everything more real.

We baked together most of the morning, until the last batch was in the oven and the first was already cool enough to eat. Annie didn't know anything; I had to teach her how to measure salt in her hand, how to punch and shape the loaves—everything. She worked hard, without saying much, but I could see that she was enjoying herself.

I found myself oddly glad of the company, too, even the company of a restless spirit. Perhaps Sara was old enough to start learning to cook, as I had learned. She wasn't much younger than I had been when Ben was born and Mother became ill. It would be nice to have company for the baking, at least. . . . I had sprinkled sliced apples and raisins on one loaf, as a treat for the children, and when the last batch was baking, I cut it, and Annie and I shared it, with fresh butter from the dairy. I was interested to see that being a ghost did not prevent her from dripping melted butter on herself as she ate.

She stopped with her mouth full of bread and put her head to one side. "Do you hear something?" she asked when she could speak.

We listened. I didn't hear anything, and said so, but Annie slipped off the bench anyway. She took off her apron and laid it across the table. "I'd better go. My mother might be worried—she wasn't sure I should come here anymore."

"Come tomorrow," I offered. "Or no, tomorrow's Sunday. But Monday's washing day, which is no fun. Well, come tomorrow, then, and I'll teach you how to make pasties. That's what I was doing the first time you visited. I've a special recipe I use that Mother got from a Cornishwoman. It's very good. Pasties were invented in Cornwall, you know."

"No, I didn't," she said. I'd thought she might like hearing about pasties, being Cornish herself, but she only smiled a little. "Good-bye, Rose."

She didn't say yes or no to making pasties with me. Perhaps she was afraid that she wouldn't be able, poor little ghost. I'd no idea what sort of restrictions were placed on her wandering, and I couldn't ask. But I didn't watch her out of sight, this time—just in case it made a difference.

Sunday was gray and cold. The children would stay indoors on a day like this, reading and playing games, and Father, too, would be resting up for his work week. I didn't really need to cook in the summer kitchen in that weather— the house could have used some heating—but somehow I found myself out there anyway, rolling out the stiff dough for the pasty crust as Mother had taught me. Pasties need a sturdy crust, if they are to stay together in a miner's lunch. I planned to slice a baby carrot or two into the potatoes and onions and rutabagas for the filling; Father would like that, and it would add a bit of color. The beef was fat enough that I didn't really need pork, but I put some in anyway, for flavor.

The air all around me was heavy and dark, filled with the tension that meant a storm was near; I kept one ear open for thunder as I worked.

Annie came as I finished crimping the crust on the first pasty and cutting it with a knife three times, so that the filling could breathe properly. Again, she was just there in the doorway. She wasn't wearing her nightgown anymore—she had on a blue jumper with a white blouse, and her hair was combed neatly back from her face and braided. And she didn't step inside.

"Annie!" I said, looking up. "You came, in spite of the storm. I'm so glad. Come in, then, before it starts to rain. Don't stand there, you'll get wet." If ghosts could get wet. She was dressed up so—perhaps because it was Sunday, for church? But it had been a Sunday the first time she'd come, too.

She looked back over her shoulder, briefly, but didn't move. "I have to go now. I just came to say good-bye. My grandmother died this morning."

"Good-bye?" A little flicker of something touched my heart. Fear? Surely not. "But we aren't finished—I haven't taught you how to make pasties yet."

"No, you haven't," she agreed. Her hands clenched against the door frame until I thought she'd give herself splinters. "I guess I'll just have to learn on my own. Because you have to leave now. Don't you?"

"Me? But—Father, the children—oh, don't be silly. I can't go anywhere."

"You can go wherever you want to go," she

said, looking at me steadily. "Your family's all grown and gone—and we even had a chance to say good-bye. Didn't we, Grandmother? I'm only sorry I couldn't come sooner. Mother is sorry, too, and even Dad. I talked to him on the phone last night, and he said he never meant—never mind. We just didn't think, any of us—but now it's done."

We stared at each other for a long, long moment. I could see the mist swirling behind her. As it parted, I caught a glimpse of a tall red-headed woman in a blue dress, looking worriedly toward the summer kitchen. Annie's mother. She seemed familiar. Like someone I had seen once, in a dream. . . .

Then I heard something else. Faintly, a voice was calling that I had never thought to hear again. I took a deep breath, understanding at last, and sorry for the burden that I had placed on this child. Or perhaps it hadn't been a burden, but a choice? I hoped so.

"Done, and past done," I said finally, feeling as if I wanted to cry. Strange to realize—we have so little time in this life. So little, and so much. "And if you didn't think, then neither did I. Thank you, child, for helping me to see—to finish. I'm glad we got to cook together, as I promised we would. And as you remembered. Tell your mother that you're to have my recipe book, if you want it. It's on the shelf in the kitchen, next to the clock. You'll find the pasty recipe in there.

Be careful—if you use too much stiffening in the crust, it will be as tough as old shoes."

She nodded, her eyes bright with tears, and she looked so much like Sara that I wanted to run to her and comfort her, but I couldn't. She was too far away. Then, as she had that first time, she melted slowly into the sunshine and mist of another daylight, somewhere I could not go anymore. As she left, for a moment I saw the summer kitchen through her eyes: an old, broken down log shed with a dusty space where the great iron stove had once stood, screens long since torn and gone, roof broken open to the sky. Through one of the half-boarded windows, I caught a glimpse of fresh green, like a garden. Then that faded, too.

In the distance I heard my mother call. "Rose! Rose Anna, my dear!"

There were others standing with her. It was time for me to go.

ABOUT THE AUTHORS

MARY DOWNING HAHN is the author of the blood-chilling and extremely popular ghost story *Wait Till Helen Comes*, which won eleven state children's choice awards. A former children's librarian, she lives in Maryland with her husband (who is still a librarian) and a black cat named Holmes.

JAMES D. MACDONALD is a former naval officer. With his wife, Debra Doyle, he has written several books for young readers, including *Knight's Wyrd* and *Bad Blood*, as well as the adult science fiction series "Mageworlds." Jim and Debra live in New Hampshire with their four children.

MICHAEL MARKIEWICZ teaches history in a private school for troubled teens. He lives in rural Pennsylvania with his wife and two "totally spastic" beagles. *The Pooka* is the second in a series of stories featuring Cai and his brother, the young king Arthur.

The first story was published in *Bruce Coville's Book of Monsters*.

MARK A. GARLAND read a copy of Arthur Clarke's *The Sands of Mars* when he was twelve and proceeded to exhaust the local library's supply of science fiction. Eventually he tried writing short stories on his own, but got sidetracked into working as a rock musician and a race car driver. Finally he came back to science fiction and has sold two novels and over two dozen short stories. Mark lives in Syracuse, New York, with his wife, their three children, and (of course) a cat.

VIVIAN VANDE VELDE lives in Rochester, New York, and mentions that her story for this book is set in that city's Mt. Hope Cemetery. She shares her house with one husband, one daughter, and one cat. She has published five fantasy novels, including *Dragon's Bait* and *User Unfriendly*.

LAWRENCE WATT-EVANS is the author of about two dozen novels of science fiction, fantasy, and horror, and about five dozen short stories. This is his first ghost story. He lives in Maryland with his wife, two kids, two cats, two hamsters, and a parakeet named Robin.

About the Authors

JANE YOLEN has published nearly a hundred and fifty books. Her work ranges from the slap-happy adventures of Commander Toad to such dark and serious stories as *The Devil's Arithmetic* to the space fantasy of her much beloved "Pit Dragon Trilogy." She lives in a huge old farmhouse in western Massachusetts with her husband, computer scientist David Stemple.

JOE R. LANSDALE is a Texas-based writer known for his unique short stories. His books include *The Drive In, The Magic Wagon*, and *Batman in: Terror on the High Skies*.

NANCY ETCHEMENDY is the author of *The Watchers of Space, The Crystal City*, and *Stranger From the Stars*. She lives in Menlo Park, California, with her husband, John, and her son, Max, who goes to a school a lot like the one she describes in "Jasper's Ghost." It is said that the green ghost of a lady haunts the school's third floor.

PATRICK BONE is a professional storyteller who has begun writing his own stories. A retired parole agent, he has also been a ranch hand, minister, policeman, prison captain, and college teacher. He lives in Littleton, Colorado, where he writes, illustrates, and teaches humanities courses at a community college.

MARY FRANCES ZAMBRENO has a doctorate in Medieval Languages and Literature. She has published two fantasy novels for young readers: *A Plague of Sorcerers* and *Journeyman Wizard*. She teaches college in the Chicago area, and does not have a cat, but wishes that she did.

JOHN PIERARD, illustrator, lives with his dogs in a dark house at the northernmost tip of Manhattan. He has illustrated *Bruce Coville's Book of Monsters*, *Bruce Coville's Book of Aliens*, and three books in the *My Teacher Is an Alien* quartet. His pictures can also be found in the popular *My Babysitter Is a Vampire* series, in the *Time Machine* books, and in *Isaac Asimov's Science Fiction* magazine.

BRUCE COVILLE was born and raised in a rural area of central New York, where he spent his youth dodging cows and chores, and dreaming of being a writer. He has always had a special interest in ghost stories, and has written four full-length novels with ghostly themes. (Three of them feature Nina Tanleven and Chris Gurley, who appear in the first story in this collection.) He now lives in a big old brick house in Syracuse, New York, with his wife, illustrator Katherine Coville, and an assortment of odd children and pets. Though he has been a teacher, a toymaker, and a gravedigger, he prefers writing. His dozens of books for young readers include the bestselling *My Teacher Is an Alien* and its sequels, as well as *Monster of the Year*, *The Ghost in the Third Row*, *The Dragonslayers*, and *Goblins in the Castle*.